TH

E1

Published by

Rainfall Books
22 Woodland Park, Calne, Wiltshire. SN11 0JX. UK.
www.rainfallsite.com

Copyright as a whole © 2017 Lines/Ford/Rainfall Books
Illustrations copyright © 2012/17 Steve Lines
Many thanks to Clive Jones for the proofreading.

All rights reserved. No part of this book may be reproduced in any form or by any means without written permission of the copyright holder, except for brief quotations in critical articles or reviews. For more information contact Rainfall Books.

FIRST EDITION PAPERBACK

1 2 3 4 5 6 7 8 9 10

RAINFALL BOOKS

ISBN 978 1976561801
CLOUD 055
Printed in the United Kingdom

The Night Eternal

BY

STEVE LINES
&
JOHN B. FORD

ILLUSTRATED BY STEVE LINES

CONTENTS

Introduction:		This, Our Voyage into Darkness by Simon Clark
1	I	The Abduction of Zareena
10	II	Khostrau
20	III	The Dungeons of Al Pharazeme
32	IV	Into the Night Eternal
48	V	The Pavilion of Sunrise
69	VI	The Sea of Sadness
85	VII	The Image of the Torturer
94	VIII	Jilyah
104	IX	The Perfumed Gardens of Death
118	X	Jeh the Beautiful
133	XI	The Valley of Silence
144	XII	The Sirens of the Night
155	XIII	The Galleries of Sublime Suffering
167	XIV	The Frozen Realm
185	XV	The Tower of the Torturer
195	XVI	Erishka: The Shadowqueen
205	XVII	Zhariman the Demon
		Glossary of Perushia
		Cartography of The Night Eternal

THIS, OUR VOYAGE INTO DARKNESS
BY SIMON CLARK

IT IS MY pleasure to introduce *The Night Eternal*. Here is an exotic and fantastical story underpinned by darkly haunting images and subtle evocation of the macabre that beautifully establishes the singular mood of the prose. The novel begins, as you will soon see, with the imagery and style of an Arabian fairy story. But swiftly it becomes a visceral action tale where scimitars flash and entrails spill bloodily to the floor. From there, we follow Khalik, our adventurer hero, as he embarks on his disturbing odyssey through 'the Demonic Realm known as The Night Eternal.'

Deliciously opulent imagery, eroticism and a swiftly unfolding plot carry the reader away on enchanted wings to mystery and excitement. Not in a long while have I read anything as vivid as this. I could almost smell the incense from smouldering frankincense, hear the beat of dragon skin drums, and feel the heat of another sun, in another kingdom, in another time…

The origins of this remarkable book intrigued me, so I asked John B. Ford if he could give me some background to its genesis. And here is what he said:-

"I think it was the late 90's when I first wrote The Night Eternal *on an old word processor, but I was never really happy with it, especially the beginning and the end of it. You won't be surprised when I tell you it was inspired by* The Night Land *and penned in the William Hope Hodgson style, but instead it details a slowly dying man's journey through a dimension in which the 'Dead' are made to suffer eternally."*

John speaks openly about his dissatisfaction with the original version of the novel. And it looked as if *The Night Eternal* was doomed to forever lie in the wasteland of old floppy discs in the bottom of the drawer. At some point, however, Steve Lines, a friend of John's, heard about the novel's moribund state and asked to read the manuscript. Steve recognized immediately that there was a wonderful treasure house of work here and persuaded John to revive it. Together, they added new story elements, polished the prose and added illustrations (created by Steve). And, thank goodness, *The Night Eternal* was rescued from oblivion.

John B. Ford is a well-respected and skilled writer of dark tales and the outré. Steve Lines is a talented visual artist, writer, and accomplished musician/ songwriter. Believe me, you are in safe hands here. Both men have the credentials to execute such a magnificent story as this one.

The novel has the poetic resonance and ambitious scope of John Bunyan's *Pilgrim's Progress* (1678). And it contains, as both John and Steve readily acknowledge, flavours of the iconic authors William Hope Hodgson, Clark Ashton Smith and Robert E. Howard. But to suggest it's a pastiche of that trio's output is simply not true. *The Night Eternal* is a vibrant, image-rich work of such visionary power that I found myself holding my breath as I turned the pages.

Here you'll find the Crimson River, together with a bridge made of human bone - and here are terrors and nightmares and dreams and adventures in a realm that lies but a heartbeat away from our own.

For some, that realm is only accessed by opening that eternal door beyond the crypt. For you, my friend, all that is required of you is to turn the page and enter the fabulous world of *The Night Eternal*.

Simon Clark, 11th June, 2010
Yorkshire.
England

The Night Eternal

Thus spoke Mazura Aharza:

"For I have created a universe where none existed. In opposition to this world which is all life, Shaizan created another which is all death, where reigns night eternal. Thus each of the marvels I have given to men for their welfare has been counteracted by a baneful gift from Shaizan. It is to him that the earth owes the evil instincts that infest it. It is he who created all the misfortunes that ravage the race of mankind. Shaizan, Lord of Night Eternal."

The Shah Nurmal - The Book of Demons

Chapter I
The Abduction of Zareena

Her forehead was flower white,
    Her cheeks like the rose, ruddy-bright,
Her eyes the captured evening light
    Shining like the crescent-moon.

The Songs of Jhal, Volume XII

THE SKY WAS heavy and dark over the jewelled spires of Sharador as I jumped from my ship just recently moored in the harbour and stared up at the glowering clouds. It was barely past midday and the looming twilight was most strange. My crew and I had beheld it as we sailed into Sharador: a dark, ominous presence that seemed to hang over the shadowed city like the death shroud of some diabolic sorcerer. And it appeared to us that this malign twilight emanated from the very walls of Sharador itself! It was an evil thing: a miasma of oppressive gloom, which obscured the sun and brought a chill to my heart. I wondered how it was possible that such transition could be wrought upon this fair city in so short a while, for it had been but ten months since we'd boarded ship and sailed from fair Sharador, voyaging to the strange and distant lands far to the east, past fabled Jaristan and out amongst the Several Seas. All had been well in the golden realm when we'd departed.

Despite this uncanny manifestation it was indeed a great joy to once more be home in Sharador, fabulous city of rare delights. But though the tarnished city did still truly shine as a jewel throughout all the lands of Perushia, never could it outshine the moon-faced visage of my true love Zareena, only daughter of Al Pharazeme blessed Caliph of Sharador, who had waited these many months for my return. My heart was intoxicated with joy and anticipation at our reunion. And oh, what tales I had to tell my love of lands both distant and exotic, for my recent adventures were marvellous beyond conjecture!

With one last quizzical glance at the twilight sky glowering above the towers and minarets of the city I ran, sandals slapping and scimitar rattling, through the winding streets and broad avenues of the city toward the palace of the Caliph where I knew Zareena awaited me, for I had sent word ahead by messenger dove that my ship approached and I would meet her in our familiar trysting place to stroll the Perfumed Gardens of Pleasure.

Presently I found myself without the Caliph's pleasure gardens and for a moment I stood and beheld the palace. Crumbling masonry showed through ivied walls; here and there fallen bricks lay amid strangling weeds; dark blemishes stained the turquoise walls of the palace and a faint air of decay lay over all. The degeneration was subtle and was not discernible at a casual glance, but it was there nonetheless and added another ambiguity to the morning.

But these were puzzles I would leave for later consideration. For there, upon a balcony festooned with fabulous brocades, filled with flowers, adorned with vases of gold and turquoise, scented with musk and amber and strewn with rubies and emeralds, I saw her who had captured my heart: the incomparable Zareena! I gazed at my beloved as she waited upon the veranda, her face flushed with excitement. She stood there silently and trembled, radiant with a beauty that would shame the Houris. But, as I made to cover the last few paces to stand beneath the balcony, I saw her turn away suddenly in an aspect of surprise and shock, her delicate hands raised to her voluptuous mouth. Fear stained the beauty of her face as she stepped rearward until she stood with her back pressed against the fretted railing, but from my low vantage point I could not perceive what it was that caused her to act thus.

Then I knew, for into view, behind her upon the balcony, appeared the loathsome shapes of three ghuls! I surmised in an instant that they sought to capture Zareena!

In less time than it takes to relate, I raced to the wall and clambered up the thick, twisted vines that girthed it, jumping onto the balcony. At a glance I saw Zareena in the paws of two of the ghuls while the third, its pallid yellow eyes glinting, turned towards me. In a moment my scimitar was free and clasped in my right hand. With one mighty lunge I thrust it deep into the hairy, matted abdomen of the approaching ghul. For a second my blade stuck fast, but with a sharp twist and a mighty wrench it slid free as the ghul let out a chilling howl and tried to grasp at its gut while its knotted, ropy entrails spilled out between its scrabbling paws. Then it fell, writhing, to the marble floor. Turning I saw the flailing form of Zareena being carried by the two remaining ghuls. One had a dirty paw covering her mouth, above which her almond, khol-lined eyes implored me to deliver her. Before I could act, the ghuls had dragged Zareena behind a large hanging tapestry. Savagely I ripped the weaving from its brackets to behold the cold, stone wall it concealed. Of Zareena, the two ghuls and a means of exit there was no sign, and thus I knew that the door had been sealed with a magical curse. There was more behind this foul abduction than provender for the loathsome ghuls. It was, I was certain, a plot of some ulterior agency. All was not well in Sharador!

* * *

I ran towards the doors of the Caliph's throne room and before the two sweating eunuchs who stood at guard either side of the ebony portal could even raise their tulwars, I had thrown the doors wide and rushed into the lofty chamber. The sight that greeted me therein caused me to stand still in disgusted horror. The air of the mighty hall was thick with pungent clouds of burning incense and myrrh, with thick and heavy odours that fogged my mind and clotted my nostrils. Amid the swirling clouds of cloying perfume I beheld a tableau of utmost depravity, for about the throne of the Caliph, in varying aspects of copulation were concubines and slaves; catamounts and courtesans; Emirs and Wazirs; Chamberlains and Nabobs; Grandees and Lords; all despoiling themselves in acts of vile fornication. Limbs twisted and entwined as the mountain of human flesh writhed, thrust, and swayed in vile acts of utter wickedness. Countless bodies were joined in lustful debaucheries and it seemed that on occasion I beheld a limb or torso or visage that appeared other than human. The wine-flushed faces of the participants were vacuous and dull as they copulated in the torrid heat of the throne room; their contorted limbs a tangle of lustful intimacy. Others lay round about the orgiastic coupling in attitudes of prone abandonment, victims of prodigal debaucheries. Other drinkers were partaking freely of the dark wine and eyeing prospective partners speculatively. Naked snake-haired dancers from far Thanarbul whirled and swayed to the lascivious throbbing of dragon skin drums, their scaled skins glistening with perspiration in the sultry heat. Eunuchs and marmalukes dispensed wine, opium, hashish and sweetmeats to the revellers who imbibed libations freely and lay about the corners and alcoves of the vast chamber in attitudes of torpor with slack faces and glazed, opium stained eyes.

Against my will I was held captured by this vile display, and so it was that many seconds passed before I turned my eyes away from the copulating forms upon the carpets and rugs, and instead gazed upon the Caliph, Al Pharazeme.

A sight no less incredible than unexpected greeted me for Al Pharazeme lolled upon his throne, absently clasping a chalice of wine in his left hand. His eyes, milk-white, the hue of rancid puss and devoid of pupils, glistened as they took in the debaucheries about him. His corpulent, slug-like form was caparisoned in soiled and stained silks and blood red wine ran from the corners of his mouth as he looked towards me and curled his lips into a smile so wicked the Daevas themselves would tremble. I could not believe that a change so dramatic could have transpired in the time I had been adventuring, for Al Pharazeme did resemble nothing more than a bloated corpse freshly wrenched from the soil. I wondered if this evil transformation of the Caliph was perchance connected in any wise with the dark pall of twilight that grew above Sharador's rooftops. His featureless white eyes shone with perverted delight as he beheld the abominable scene about him and I gazed upon his grey and decaying visage in profound astonishment. The changes time had wrought upon the Caliph were marked beyond understanding. His skeletal hands, with long, wicked fingernails, black and curling, gripped the arms of his throne as he looked upon me. His mottled flesh, seeped and sweated a disgusting puss, the sickly odour of which the heady perfumes and spices could not completely mask – it was the stagnant odour of decay. Gone was the clean-eyed, ruddy-faced visage I remembered of old and in its place a cadaver that lived and breathed! Of a surety all was not well in Sharador for there was evil magic here.

Then, standing behind and to the right of the throne, I beheld the form of Khostrau, the conjurer. He stood; arms folded across his breast, face impassive, clad in flowing robes of purple silk, trimmed with yellow, which fell in billowing folds to the floor. His amber eyes betrayed no emotion and his old and wrinkled face, scarcely visible in the mane of white hair and beard that tumbled down his chest, remained frozen as I gazed upon it. I wondered what changes time and circumstance had wrought in my old friend, for his appearance remained as I remembered it, though sterner of aspect, and his eyes were inscrutable and cold as the starless void. They remained downcast and would not meet mine.

A sudden and disconcerting breeze blew from the direction of the shadowed alcove behind and to the left of the Caliph's throne. Carried with it came a faint sibilation, like the whispering of some evil Daeva intent on future slaughter. Abruptly it ceased, and for the first time I perceived the Caliph had a new Grand Vizier. He stood amongst shadows, which cloaked his form like the fretted wings of demons. His black-shrouded form seemed to represent the height of formidable authority and mystique. His face I could not discern for, from the loose cowl about his head, was pinned an ebon veil of silk that masked his features. Yet this veil was not an obstruction to the vision of the Grand Vizier, it was a surety, for even now he faced my direction in obvious scrutiny. Then he turned and walked silently into the embracing gloom.

Once more my eyes turned to the Caliph, as a rattling cough escaped his rotting mouth. Then he spoke through vocal chords of dust and decayed skin, the remnants of pale lips moving to produce a bizarre, almost threatening voice that surely had no right to speak:

"O mighty Khalik, adventurer and explorer of the Several Seas, I salute your return to Sharador. Sit awhile and regale us with fine tales of your latest voyage."

His voice was cold and rasping and a chill gripped my spine as I began to surmise that Al Pharazeme somehow already knew of Zareena's abduction. Bowing and kissing the ground between my hands I addressed the disgusting creature that occupied the throne:

"O mighty Al Pharazeme, Caliph and most splendid ruler of Sharador the Golden, I bring news most dire! This very hour your beloved daughter Zareena has been abducted by loathsome ghuls from the very balconies of your palace!"

At this the Caliph's eyes narrowed, but he spoke not.

I continued: "I managed to slay one of the foul creatures, spilling its stinking guts upon the marble floor, but two more of the fiends spirited Zareena away through a hidden door, which was then sealed with a magical curse."

Al Pharazeme's eyes looked to the floor, and in an instant I knew that Zareena's abduction was not only known to him, but it was a surety that he had also played some clandestine part in the foul deed. Anger blossomed within me like a black lotus:

"A thousand curses upon you! Would you not deliver your only child from the clutches of these evil fiends? We must make haste and trace these beasts to their den!"

Al Pharazeme raised his sunken, insipid eyes towards mine and within them I beheld madness lurking like a crouching demon.

"My Healing is now complete, Khalik, sailor of the Several Seas. Shaizan is the Healer; my expiration was not truly the end for Death is now my own domain. You too could rule in this Domain of Death. I would that you forget Zareena, for her soul is corrupted and cursed and she cannot be redeemed. Join me in the coming New Age of Darkness and rule my glorious armies of Death!"

I gazed at Al Pharazeme in abject horror and at these loathsome words my anger did spill over into violent action. I drew my scimitar, still stained with the dark blood of the ghul I had killed and made to slay the abominable creature that lolled upon the throne. Whereupon I beheld Khostrau wave a languid hand and mumble a *Word* and darkness overtook me. As I slipped into unconsciousness I heard the Caliph's mocking laughter . . .

Chapter II
Khostrau

"You are human beings, masters of the world. In the perfection of thought I have created you the first creatures. Think that which is good, say that which is good, do that which is good. Do not worship Shaizan."

The Shah Nurmal, Book III

WITH CONSCIOUSNESS RETURNING to me, I immediately reached for my sword, yet this I found was not in its scabbard but had been laid upon the floor at my right-hand side. In an instant I saw that I reposed on fine Perushian carpets within a small bedchamber. Silk curtains obscured the entrance. I arose, sword in hand and with caution slowly parted the hangings and entered the chamber beyond. There, awaiting me stood Khostrau! I raised my scimitar and lunged at the foul traitor, but with a subtle twisting of his fingers Khostrau's sorcerous powers held me immobile.

"Greetings Khalik! Did you think an old friend had betrayed you? Had I not rendered you unconscious Al Pharazeme would have had you slain before you'd but moved an inch. You've doubtless observed the changes that have occurred within and without the palace? Well there is much to tell, but know you that the Caliph and his Grand Vizier have strange powers, powers against which your sword, however sharp, is no match. Al Pharazeme has commanded that I subject you to subtle tortures and then return you to his chamber to join his debaucheries."

At these words I strained with all possible effort to free myself from Khostrau's magical conjuring, but with no success.

"Fear not, Khalik", continued Khostrau, "as I say, an old friend has not deserted you. Words do not always match the deed. I do not intend to torment you beyond the suffering that you endure knowing that Zareena has been abducted. Rather I intend to give you your liberty and answer the many questions you doubtless have, for there have been a lot of changes in Sharador, since last you were here."

Indeed it was so! For I felt the invisible bonds slacken and I was again able to move once more. Cautiously I sheathed my scimitar and Khostrau gestured to a low divan, upon which I sat. He lowered his old and twisted frame into a strangely contorted chair of black jade and spoke:

"Listen, Khalik, Sailor of the Several Seas, to the tale of The Healing of Al Pharazeme. Know that it is related that Al Pharazeme was the son of Al Kaloor and the grandson of Al Ishakar and is seventh Caliph of the wondrous municipality of Sharador, capital city of these fabled lands of Perushia.

"Now Al Pharazeme was not perforce a wicked man, for his early days as Caliph of Sharador were benign and laced with wisdom, as you are aware. His rule was just, his laws strict but fair and all in Sharador and the lands of Perushia prospered mightily. The people rejoiced and all was well in the land. But, with your departure from Sharador, came Zinshaz to the palace. Whence he came, none can say, but scarce were your billowed sails sunk beneath the shimmering horizon when he stood before the throne of Al Pharazeme, which, in the manner of Suloman, is flanked by black panthers of ebony and jade. Now Zinshaz offered to cook the Caliph a banquet of twenty courses and his culinary skills were such that Al Pharazeme was so delighted with the exquisite quality and flavour of the dishes consequently prepared that he offered to reward Zinshaz, saying he could receive as a gift anything he desired within the realm of Perushia, save his only daughter, the fair Zareena. Zinshaz smiled and asked only that he be appointed Grand Vizier and be allowed to advise the Caliph on delicate matters of state, and perchance cook an occasional meal for his magnificence. To this the Caliph heartily agreed and thus it was that Al Pharazeme sealed his doom.

"In time Zinshaz taught the Caliph to eat the flesh of animals, and unknown to him, the flesh of humans also, for his skills in the kitchen were glorious and the dishes well spiced and flavoured. So it was that the Caliph became corrupted and the customs of decent men vanished and the desires of the wicked Zinshaz were accomplished. Thus he began to transform the Caliph into a redoubtable demon. Ever was Zinshaz at the Caliph's left-hand side; whispering; guiding; manipulating, until it was that in the court of Sharador, virtue was despised and vice flaunted itself openly. And at all times his Grand Vizier stood at Al Pharazeme's side and whispered poisonous words into his ear, ever urging him to greater and more awful acts of decadence and debasement.

"As the months passed the Caliph's indulgences and dissipations caused him to fall most ill and despite their ministrations there was naught the palace physicians could do for him. And so it was that Al Pharazeme did retreat to his chambers and took to his deathbed. It was but four months gone that he commanded all to leave his bedchamber and summoned Zinshaz to his side, who arrived silently, his features hidden by his ebon mask and, alone, the pair remained within the chambers throughout the dark night. Marmalukes and eunuchs heard strange noises emanating from within; sonorous invultations followed by appalling screams and shrieks. These endured throughout the long night but ceased abruptly with the coming of the dawn. Presently, to the consternation of all within the palace, the Caliph emerged, looking pale and drawn and presenting the aspect of a corpse, but with eyes bright (though, it was noted with horror, white and featureless). What transpired within those walls there is none who knows, though there are some who talk of consort with vile demons, but the Caliph claimed to have been 'healed' of the 'affliction of death', though what that may mean I cannot say with any surety. He then commanded that all should celebrate his wondrous 'healing' and so it was that he embarked upon his endless orgy of decadence and dissolution.

"Thus it was that you found him Khalik, degenerate and depraved and sitting by unmoving amid orgiastic excess while his only daughter is captured by ghuls and spirited away."

As Khostrau finished his tale I said:

"But how is it that you stood by and did nothing throughout the decline of the Caliph, surely your magic could have saved him?"

"There was naught I could do Khalik, for Zinshaz is more than he seems. My familiars have revealed to me that he is none other than Zhariman himself, the Demon Lord of The Night Eternal! My meagre conjurings cannot prevail against such as he, for my soul would be surely forfeit if I stood against him. I have long known of Zhariman's deception, but if he were to have sensed that I was aware of him, he would have destroyed me in an instant, despite my power. It has shattered my heart to see the changes wrought upon the Caliph and the kingdom by Zhariman's poison, but naught could I do but pretend allegiance to the Caliph. Zhariman suspects, I'm sure, but weightier matters occupy his mind, not least of which is your long expected return to Sharador, for I sense you have a part to play in his cunning plans.

"Al Pharazeme has been 'healed' of the affliction of death by the demonic powers of Zhariman and his master Shaizan and I am confident that the price for this 'healing' was the pure soul of Zareena. I can but conclude that Zhariman has caused her to be taken to his own realm, The Night Eternal, but for what purpose I know not!"

"But that I had arrived moments earlier," I replied, "for then it would have been a somewhat different tale!" I fingered my blade, my eyes grim and hard. "The vengeance I exact upon Zhariman will be legendary!"

"Indeed, but you have much to learn of the Night Eternal before you begin Khalik, though I know you yearn to be gone and avenge yourself upon the Demon Lord. There are many dangers within His domain, and the tales I told you and Zareena in your youth do but barely touch upon them. Take you to the Great Library and peruse the *Shah Nurmal, the Book of Demons,* for it contains much on the Death Realm that would help you, but return to me at midnight. And remember Khalik; trust no one."

"I will trust no one," I replied.

* * *

And so I left Khostrau to his tortured thoughts and made my way to the Great Library. Yet it was upon my journey there I chanced to glance out through a window and was alarmed to see that darkness had already begun to shroud the view of the palace gardens and the streets of Sharador, for it was but only mid afternoon.

Presently, I arrived at the library and for some hours I studied the ancient pages of the *Shah Nurmal,* and so read much concerning the demonic realm known as The Night Eternal, though still occasionally gazing through a nearby window at all the mystery of the ever looming twilight. The sun shone as a dull orange disc and I could not help but wonder if the end of all things was approaching, for each time I looked, I saw no trace of obstacle to obscure its light, and to me that dull orange orb now seemed to be dying. Gazing through the window once again I noticed, in the twilight shadows of the gardens, there moved a small circle of radiance, and within it I discerned the veiled figure of Zinshaz, who I now knew to be Zhariman, the Demon Lord, walking slowly. What he used for illumination I could not espy, though it seemed to be some manner of white flower. As I watched, my anger blossomed like a black lotus as I beheld the evil Demon Lord, yet still I held it in check with an iron will, for I dare not slay the foul creature 'till Zareena was once again safe within my arms.

And so, with a whispered curse I returned to my studies, all the while aching to be on my way to rescue Zareena and destroy Zhariman, but in all my perusing of the *Shah Nurmal* I had found no clue as to how to obtain entry into the cursed realm of The Night Eternal. For this knowledge Khostrau alone possessed.

In the early evening I heard the swish of silk, and so looking up from my studies I saw, by the glow of my lamp, that the concubine Varuni had entered the library. In silence she walked to my side, and from a silver tray, deposited upon my desk many rare fruits and wines of Samarzul and Zaraby, smiling as she did so. This done she departed, momentarily stopping by my window, with her pale face looking upwards at the gathering darkness. In the flickering shadows of the lamp, it seemed to me that her breast rose and fell in silent weeping or laughter.

After I had eaten my fill of the welcome repast, I read again from the *Shah Nurmal,* but with each paragraph it seemed that a tremendous fatigue clawed at my mind and weighed heavily upon my eyes. Finally I gave way to the desire for sleep, meaning to rest for an hour or so on my carpets, which I had placed in a corner between two towering shelves laden with rare volumes. I laid myself down upon my bed and my consciousness travelled to the place of deepest black.

The lamp was burning low when I awoke, but still it threw enough light for me to see that the hour must have passed midnight. My body felt like ice, my muscles frozen almost rigid, and I rose up from my bed only with the greatest difficulty. Walking to an alcove, I took out another lamp and lighted it. This I carried with me as I left the library, groggily walking back along the darkened corridors of the palace to Khostrau's chambers.

* * *

When I again entered Khostrau's room, I saw that anger and impatience had bestowed upon him the terrible aspect of a Jinni.

"You are late!"

"Forgive me Khostrau, for after my evening repast I was given to a fatigued sleep the like of which I have never before known."

Khostrau gave a strangulated sob of disbelief and shock. His trembling hand reached towards me and his burning gaze seemed to pierce my soul.

"Khalik, did I not tell you, trust no one? Do you not know what Zhariman has done to you? Just as he drains the very light from the skies of Perushia; so he now drains the life from you. Your soul is encased within a poisoned shell that every moment grows colder."

Khostrau's words caused a chill of horror within me. "But how?" I asked.

"Have you not guessed, Khalik? Zhariman corrupted you when you ate the food he offered."

I did not understand. "But my food was brought to me by Varuni," I explained.

"Another of his deceptions; Varuni is within the Caliph's Seraglio. The concubines are forbidden to leave its environs. You were visited by a Druj, in the service of the Demon Lord."

"Then I am to become as Al Pharazeme?" I said in horror, and slowly lowered my hand to clasp his, while icy tears formed within my eyes.

"No, it is not a surety," replied Khostrau, "Zhariman has merely forced our next course of action. True your body becomes colder, rigid of muscle, and hard to articulate and to stay much longer within *this* realm will result in the coming of death to you, aye and more than death."

"Then what must I do, Khostrau?"

"Evil stalks the palace of the Caliph, Khalik, and as the acts of Al Pharazeme have become more and more debased, so this infernal twilight has grown. It breeds and thrives within the very air of the palace and as Al Pharazeme's corruption touches and corrupts others, so the twilight grows. The palace is the heart of corrupted evil, which is ever spreading to the city without and, in time will seep into the lands beyond, into Samarzul and Illonia and Harakash, until all Perushia will know the cold kiss of the evil which breeds here. Even now the sun is dulled and twilight lengthens to grasp the wrists of dawn."

"This unholy twilight is the work of Zhariman?"

"Indeed it is so," continued Khostrau, "for Zhariman fans the dark flames with his conjurings and his false promises and as Al Pharazeme corrupts all about him so the evil spreads.

"We are heading towards a world of darkness. These are the days of Falling Night and there are hungry eyes in all that dark. The Night Eternal will fall upon the world and thus the power of Zhariman will grow and strengthen. Monsters and Jinn will flow from the darkness attracted by the stench of humanity, to feed and frolic in the new lands of Death.

"What you must do, Khalik, is that which you most desire. You must enter the Night Eternal and destroy the heart of Zhariman. A heart so black that from it pours all the darkness of the Night Eternal. It will not be an easy task, for even now Zhariman returns to his Dark Realm there to await your coming. You are to play some covert part in his malign plans and I suspect that his abduction of Zareena and the tainting of your soul are just incentives to give surety that you enter his nightmare realm. The Demon Lord awaits you, Khalik."

At these words I smiled a grim smile: "It shall be his undoing, for I shall slay the Demon Lord and rescue Zareena!" And indeed my sluggish heart did beat hard within my breast as I uttered these words, for I deemed it a surety that I would kill Zhariman and rescue Zareena, or else die in the attempt!

Chapter III
The Dungeons of Al Pharazeme

We are the damned that Death has cursed,
Our souls are chained by Hate.
The tortured ones who cannot die,
In constant torment wait.

Al Pharazeme has cheated Death,
For Death can never die.
He feeds upon all suffering,
Drinks deep the tortured cry.

The Songs of Jhal, Volume XII

WE LEFT THE chambers of Khostrau and, avoiding the guards and spies of the Caliph, walked through many corridors of darkness and dust and made our way to the east wing of the palace, for here it was, said the conjurer, that entry to the Dark Realm lay.

Presently we arrived at a disused chamber deep within the bowels of the palace and stood at the top of a winding stone staircase, this plunging down to the dungeons of the Caliph far below. But it was as we approached the head of that sinister staircase that I was shaken by a moment of great astonishment and fear, for I saw that the decent was illuminated! Fire torches hung from the walls at regular intervals; beacons of light in the gloom. They snaked downwards as though set there for the very purpose of guiding us to that nightmare realm. But was I, in this body of coldness with weakening heart, still truly a child of life? And who could more belong beneath the earth than I? Then my thoughts turned to tortured spirits, souls of darkness and the putrid stench of death.

Khostrau remained silent as we slowly began to descend the uneven marble steps, but still I knew his eyes were constantly observing my face. I detected a sorrow there, deeper than the chasm of Sindroo.

In due course we came to the bottom of the flight of stairs. Dampness hung in the air and I could hear the ceaseless drip of water. Dank mists lent eerie shimmerings to dim wall-lanterns, while the sound of scurrying rats within the darkness echoed down the dismal corridor before us and conjured unwelcome thoughts of hungry ghuls with lambent eyes aflame with evil desire.

Along that noisome corridor I walked with Khostrau, with it being many moments before I broke the oppressive silence with a question.

"Khostrau, who has lit the way to the dungeons?"

"Zareena's captors," Khostrau replied, "for it is the wish of Zhariman that you enter his realm to liberate Zareena."

"But are not the dungeons of Al Pharazeme always kept secured?"

"There are no locks for Zhariman," said Khostrau, "you will find the entrance to the Tombs of Torture now lie open."

And the words he spoke were then proved to be true, for when I pressed the weight of my body against the forbidding door which marked the entrance to the chambers we sought, it mournfully opened, allowing our access to a malign realm of unparalleled suffering; a place which surely could have only been envisaged by the depraved mind of a madman.

Within, a host of manacled corpses hung suspended from the slime encrusted stone walls; while from the throat of each dying body there protruded a pipe of frosted crystal. Each pipe led to large crystalline troughs, all carrying a constant flow of noisome blood. I tried to imagine what kind of sorcery could maintain such a flow, and to my mind came the image of a large black heart steadily pumping and sucking within the confines of some foul subterranean chamber.

I was sickened and appalled as Khostrau and I walked through chamber after chamber all displaying a similar tableau. On occasion, bodies of waning life looked upon us with doleful faces and weeping eyes, pleading for help.

As we continued to descend, I noticed the crystalline troughs were pumping their crimson contents down to putrid lakes of blood. The immense size of the dungeons then struck me for the first time, and I became curious, wondering who had built and maintained such a place of ultimate nightmare.

"How large are the dungeons of the Caliph, Khostrau?" I asked.

"More vast than can ever be fathomed! Their myriad tunnels stretch out beyond imagining."

"But how could such a creation ever come to be?"

Khostrau looked me straight in the eyes, coughed, and seemed to hesitate a little before going on.

"The original dungeons were as nothing to these shadowed chambers; these were fashioned in the months you have spent a voyaging, magically created by jinn, to pander to the darker obsessions of Al Pharazeme. The Demon's influence on the Caliph was devastating, as you have witnessed. His lusts grew more depraved until it seemed that no abomination was beyond him. Zhariman caused the dungeons to be built at Al Pharazeme's request so that the Caliph could indulge his sick desires, extending the original dungeons on a colossal scale and eventually bringing about this bizarre creation from the deepest region of his poisonous brain. Ah, Khalik, I see you have failed to comprehend that this dark creation is but a mocking image of the exquisite horrors which await you in the Night Eternal."

I was astounded by these words of Khostrau's, for I had not realised the true extent of the power which the Demon held over Al Pharazeme and never would I have believed that such pure evil could exist within Al Pharazeme's tainted soul. We continued to walk, continually passing pools of rancid blood lit by circles of black candles. Shrouded figures knelt in silence around the edges of these pools; their ashen faces expectantly studying each surface. Other dark figures walked in solemn processions, their shoulders carrying corpses freshly exhumed and soiled with graveyard sludge; then the thought occurred to me that here was a place where life could never belong, for this was indeed a Domain of

Death. Then the dry voice of Khostrau spoke in anticipation of a question I was about to ask.

"All the dead are in the employ of the Demon; they need no sustenance or slumber, and require no monetary payment."

"But is there no hope beyond death; are we not destined for Paradise?" I spoke angrily.

"This I do not deny, but in *this place* the fight for life can never be won and will only bring prolonged suffering and thus much enjoyment to the vile minds of Al-Pharazeme and his evil master. There is no hope for these wretched creatures we see before us."

We had now reached a vast underground cavern. From a tunnel opening to our left a crimson river flowed gently through the chamber to vanish into the gloom. In the near distance I saw two dim figures aboard a shallop captured in an eerie radiance, the source of which I could not discern. The larger of the figures ceased rowing as they entered the gaping black mouth of the large tunnel and turned towards me, and, just for a second, I felt myself held in a formidable gaze of immense power. Not far from where we stood, another wooden shallop was moored to a rusty iron rail above crumbling stone steps that descended to the river's edge. Within the interior of the shallop there had been placed a low-burning lamp of burnished silver, its constantly flickering shadows giving the illusion of a sinister, floating tomb -- and the death-throes of a faceless occupant.

I knew this river from my readings in the library of Khostrau.

"Khostrau, this is Zirik Mobol! Zhariman has taken Zareena away from us, taken her down the Crimson River of Death!"

His wrinkled face displayed no sign of shock, but deep sorrow shone in the wells of his eyes as he whispered, "I have failed Sharador..."

"No, Khostrau!" I exclaimed.

"I should have acted when I recognised Zinshaz for the Demon Lord, Zhariman," continued Khostrau. "He will corrupt Zareena and initiate her into the Dark Way. Perhaps if I had loved her more, if I had protected her, she would still be safe! Her heart will soon share the darkness of the Demon's own. You must save her Khalik"

* * *

Khostrau motioned for me to follow and we walked alongside the Crimson River following the current, betimes seeming to glimpse smooth white creatures moving just beneath the foamy surface. Now a rapid flow had begun, and it was with some intrigue that I saw each whitened form commence to struggle frantically against it. Looking at Khostrau's face, I saw it now wore a saddened aspect, while on his cheeks tears glistened in the light of the nearest fire-torch.

"Souls of bodies, unfortunate ones, I pray for you," he muttered.

With these words I came to a terrible understanding. And so, quickly averting my eyes away from the cruel suffering before me, I quietly whispered my own words of holy blessing. Then, in the following seconds, there came a potent increase in the anger I felt against Zhariman, and the pity I felt for poor, helpless Zareena.

Now, in some short while we came upon the sight of a white bridge, many eyes of fire burnt through the gloomy dark as its occupants constantly studied our approach. When we grew nearer, their faces of pale-white became clearer to our eyes. For built with a cruel and twisted skill, this bridge of whitened bone incorporated a macabre row of skulls in its design, the inside of each lit by its own black candle. Then, with a most sudden and terrible dawning, I realised this was Gorannon, named in the *Shar Nurmal* as the Skull-lit Bridge of Evil. And so fearfully we began to cross over this morbid structure, for our way was now illuminated by the unseeing dead, candlelight flickering eerily through hollow eye sockets.

"How could the Demon ever conceive of such a monstrosity?" I asked.

Khostrau answered without meeting my eyes, his voice held the quality of deepest shame.

"This is not the work of Zhariman," he replied.

* * *

As I stepped from the bridge I heard a faint whisper leave Khostrau's lips.

"And now I must pray it still exists -- that the Demon never fathomed the use to which I put it."

"Of what do you speak?" I asked.

"I speak of my only act of defiance against the tyranny of Zhariman. I speak of the Keseva, Pool of Purification -- that which separates soul from body."

Before us there stood a small pyramid of polished onyx, scarce twenty paces in width and an equal measurement in height. Ebon draperies hung over a central entranceway, and planted in my mind was a sudden vision of the veil of Zinshaz. Khostrau detected a shudder in me as we walked towards it.

"Sometimes the greatest of good can come from that which is created by evil. Follow me within the chamber!"

As I stepped through the veils I was hit by a sudden blast of heated air. My skin stung as though pierced by a thousand needles and I staggered, barely able to withstand the pain.

Khostrau's sardonic laughter rang loud through clouds of crimson vapour.

"Ah, such irony," he said, "for a purely mortal man would have been seared to a cinder by the Vapours of Purification, but your tainted soul welcomes the kiss of the Crimson Breath."

"Are you not mortal?" I asked

"Yes, but my flesh is protected by potent sorceries", replied Khostrau.

"Do I still live?" I asked.

"Yes," Khostrau's sad eyes studied me, "you still live, but already you are embracing the undying death of the Night Eternal. For you there is no turning back, even should you wish it."

I smiled grimly and clutched the hilt of my scimitar tightly. It was not my intention to abandon my quest until Zareena lay in my arms and the black heart of the Demon Lord was stilled forever!

Khostrau smiled sadly at my expression of resolve and gestured into the mist. Then I saw the small pool in the centre of the chamber.

"The water of the Lake of Ibliz, mixed with the blood of Man, diluted with the tears of Jinn. This, O Khalik, is what you see before you. So simple, and yet so very potent that its red vapours leap in the air to kiss your face with tender fire. Unbeknown to the Demon, I have used this pool to release many souls from their cages of death."

I gazed at the crimson pool within the mist. "And the Demon uses this Pool of Purification for other means?"

"You saw evidence of the ghastly use he makes of it within Zirik Mobol," continued Khostrau, "souls swept into realms of everlasting dark and eternal torture. The guilt of it all continually gnaws at me, for I stood by and allowed Al Pharazeme to fall under the spell of this demonic monstrosity who drinks the very light of the world; one who will slowly drain the life from every living form within Perushia."

"And we are powerless?" I asked. "Powerless to halt the black tendrils of this evil scheme which the Demon has set into motion?"

Khostrau's intelligent eyes blinked.

"As I did previously relate, the death of Perushia can only be prevented by the destruction of the Demon's heart. Khalik, oh my brother, you are the Chosen One; through your own carelessness he has poisoned you and now drains not just your own life, but your very soul. I warned you to trust no one -- and yet you blindly ate and drank 'nourishment' supplied by Zhariman. Upon your shoulders alone must ride the last hope of all Perushia."

"And the Demon knows I will follow him?"

"He expects it. You saw for yourself that he has made a shallop ready for you. He derives pleasure from torment and suffering, and so would have you enter the Night Eternal with body and soul intact. He is prepared to trade the slightest peril for the gratification of observing your struggles and suffering. And now must I make use of the Pool of Purification one final time."

I gazed into the eyes of Khostrau and saw the pain and guilt that resided there. He spoke again:

"Once my purification is complete, Khalik, you must put me from your mind and depart at once to follow the Crimson River of Death."

He indicated with his eyes that I should move myself away from the pool, which he slowly walked towards, pausing at the edge of its crimson contents. Suddenly there came a low moan from his lips and the red liquid directly beneath his feet began to bubble and splash upwards towards him. Observing this I became repulsed and afraid, for the crimson fluid commenced to climb the hem of Khostrau's robe, like probing fingers. I watched, helpless, while the conjurer began to struggle and squirm with frenzied movement as the sentient liquid groped steadily upwards, until it appeared that Khostrau was clad in living robes of scarlet. His lips parted as if to speak to me, but before he could make utterance, the red fluid rippled, pulsed and thrust its way obscenely into his mouth and down his throat, stifling both speech and breath. In a frenzied spasm the body of Khostrau tottered forward and splashed deep into the crimson pool, his mouth now free once more, was open and sucking in gulps of bubbling red fluid. Then came the screams; screams of agony such as I had never before heard, not even in my many dangerous exploits around the Several Seas, for skin and bone began to bubble and dissolve into a putrescent, milky-white liquid, this creating a nauseating contrast against the red. At this sight all I could do was step back and bury my head in my hands, for I was unable to bear the sight of such suffering in one I had called friend.

* * *

After some while all was silent. Dreading what next I would witness, I uncovered my eyes to see the last traces of a greasy white stain disappear beneath a calm surface of crimson. And so for some moments I stood meditating in deep sorrow, then my thoughts, ever questioning, wondered whether the will of Zhariman had infiltrated Khostrau's mind, causing him to bring himself to such an agonising end. More minutes of silence passed in which the pool showed a curious rippling upon its surface and occasional unexplained splashes. Then the memory of Khostrau's last words echoed through my head.

So I left the Pool of Purification, walking away in a state of numbed shock and deep melancholy. And in some short while I came once more to the Skull-lit Bridge of Evil that spanned Zirik Mobol, but now the presence of a chill wind sighed and moaned around that strange structure, like airy spirits of the dead in vengeful mood. With this, I wondered how such gusts as these could possibly be present within lower-level dungeons. Yet still I stepped onto that nightmare edifice and began to walk its course, for I thought me to discover another means of entry to the Night Eternal rather than take the offered shallop and become a plaything of the Demon Lord. But when I was but halfway along its frightful span that direful wind began to howl so darkly that it seemed to me the Edimmu, the avenging souls of all the dead, moaned in grim satisfaction. And in the following seconds I came to be gripped by the icy fist of fear, for one by one the candles of each skull flickered and were extinguished, as though caught in the breath of some baleful demon. Darkness smothered me like a clinging death-shroud, and I reached out, gripping the rail of bone with shaking hands to gain my balance.

From the far side of the bridge I then discerned the sudden startling sound of echoing footsteps and two orbs of fire lit the darkness, never once blinking in their thorough scrutiny of my very soul. And as that malign vision grew nearer, I drew my scimitar and stood ready to face whatever denizen of this foul underworld approached.

Suddenly a leprous green lit the outline of an emaciated figure clad in tattered rags, worn slippers and soiled turban and a large tulwar thrust inside a wide sash. The figure halted to stand before me and eyes of luminous jade flame burnt from beneath his brows to cleave the darkness and peer deep into my own dark eyes, while putrid snatches of breath hinted at the internal decay from a soul of blackness. To my face he lifted a cold skeletal hand, and before I could react in any manner my consciousness was drained to the hollow echoes of unholy laughter.

Chapter IV
Into the Night Eternal

Ghul and Jinn and evil sprite
Shall keep me company tonight,
For Zirik Mobol draws me nigh
The land where Death can never die.

Zal in the Land of Demons

I AWOKE TO DISCOVER I had been laid upon my back, arms folded across my chest. My first action upon returned consciousness was to check for my scimitar, and with this I was taken with much surprise, for it still remained safely within its scabbard, strapped about my waist. Despite this there grew in me a feeling of disconcertion, and as my blurry vision cleared I studied my surroundings. Many eerie, flickering shadows caused by a constantly dancing flame from a delicately carved silver lamp played over me and evoked comparison in my memory of the deadly black serpents that grew from the shoulders of Zohar in ancient legend. Following this a sudden realisation dawned in me that I reposed inside the shallop. Rising up, I saw Zirik Mobol, the Crimson

River of Death, now carried me in its rapid flow; vague white forms occasionally breaking its vermilion surface in frenzied struggle. While looking before me in the distant gloom, I beheld the awesome sight of Shotu, the Tunnel of Darkness, looming, and with this I knew great trepidation. For if the writings within the *Shah Nurmal* were truth then traversing the passageway would make me the first owner of a living soul to experience the forbidden sights within the Realm of Death, for Shotu was the secret gateway to the Night Eternal!

Now as I approached the jaws of the tunnel, it came to my notice that the lamp I had been afforded was now burning low on oil and would soon be extinguished. This observation was soon proved to be accurate for as I plunged into the darkness and cold of that unholy place, it was with faltering heart that I saw its final flame sputter and die. Then a sinister crypt-like blackness enveloped me.

Travelling on through the darkness of the tunnel, there slowly crept over me a feeling of terrible menace, almost as though the structure through which I ventured was incredibly hostile. For it seemed to me to be a vast construction of abominable intelligence and power. Still I travelled on, carried within the fierce flow of Zirik Mobol, and with every passing second there grew in me the conviction that my life was threatened by some imminent danger. For of a surety in all my fantastic voyages upon the Several Seas I had never felt so vulnerable and afraid, and at that moment I could have sworn some hidden form of malevolence had grown very near.

Then something touched me from the darkness above.

In my mind I envisioned the yellow fingernails of a ghul raking through my hair: one in the employ of Zhariman, meaning to snatch me from life. But with the continuance of the sensation my sense returned and reaching up through the darkness I felt a concave roof of stone and it was this that my hair had swept against. At this, I made search of the shallop to seek the paddles, finding them lying beside me, for now an appalling thought had of a sudden entered my mind. I then purposely dragged one paddle along to the starboard and the shallop veered only for some very short distance before hitting a wall of solid stone. Repeating the procedure upon the opposing side I quickly obtained the same devastating result, and then I knew for a surety that the roof and walls of the tunnel were narrowing about me.

For some while I attempted to row against the current of the river, but this quickly proved fruitless, for the strength of the unholy river proved to be much too powerful. In the following seconds the ceiling began to further close down upon me and I realised I would very soon be forced to again lie horizontally in the shallop. Moving with the natural instinct of survival, I flung myself over the port side of the shallop with all my bodily weight, in the same instant pulling down with all the strength of my sailor's arms in an attempt to overturn the craft. Following this came the sudden scraping of wood against stone, and the small boat turned to capsize over me.

Beneath it I now grasped hold of the planking which had formerly been my seat, taking breaths from that pocket of air created by the upturned boat, and when the roof descended, meaning to drown me, I laughed to myself and knew I had outwitted Zhariman in this first test of my wits.

For some minutes I travelled beneath the shallop, carried by the flow of Zirik Mobol toward the realm of Eternal Night.

Then I felt the boat begin to rise.

* * *

I broke through the surface of crimson, taking in deep breaths and thinking to fill my lungs with pure air -- but instead I became sickened. For all about me the atmosphere was redolent with stagnant odours of decay. The pungent stench of corruption was carried upon the breeze, and now my surroundings were beyond the dark imaginings of any man. So I swam to the nearest shore, which lay to my left, and pulled myself from the river. I got to my feet and looked about me with more apprehension and fear than surely any man has ever known. A sombre landscape of blackness filled my vision; occasional eruptions of fire lent light to the vision of nightmare. Before me a bleak valley stretched as far as the eye could determine; I espied the eerie outline of sinister leafless trees that swayed to a breeze of melancholy sighs, and the thought came to me that I now listened to the plaintive sighings of all the dead.

To my far right, a mountainous region was lit by occasional columns of livid fire, which struck up into the night-black sky; like accusing fingers of flame, they seemed to stab upwards at the ebon skies with demonic hatred. And right in the midst of the nearest mountain, was a darksome opening into which Zirik Mobol fiercely flowed, carrying my abandoned, upturned shallop.

Now, it was as I was taken with the study of my surroundings, that I was suddenly amazed to detect a brief flicker of light, which lit the blackness of the void above. And so looking upwards, I studied the heavens with a great intensity, but not one sign of starlight did I see. Though as I continued to gaze, there suddenly came to me the sight of Baul, the pale opal moon, which shone down through fretted clouds of black. Beams of silver light fell upon this thrice-accursed land, and bathed the scarlet water of Zirik Mobol in its departure from the Tunnel of Darkness.

And at this sight I knew the cold grip of fear, for all the darkness within the tunnel shrank away from the light -- as though to show me plainly the interior. Then I felt no shame at my dread, for that narrowed tunnel which had only moments before threatened my very life, would now have allowed access to my own fully-rigged ship which lay in Sharador's harbour. Then I realised the nature of the pure evil and cruelty that dwelt within this realm of Everlasting Night, so that I knew of a surety that all the land was an extension of the will of Zhariman; alive and ever aware of my intrusion.

And thus it was that I began my journey through this land of death and strangeness. Having no knowledge of what evil may lie concealed within the dark, I determined that to remain within a place of easy observation was doubtless to invite great danger. So carefully I began to walk across the blackened ground, and making my destination the mountainous region to my right. But as I walked steadily across the arid landscape, the eerie breeze once more sighed plaintively through the branches of those grotesque trees. Each tree stood as though frozen, and just for a second I entertained the absurd notion that they sighed with sadness to see me, a man of life, enter into such an accursed region.

Within a short while the land began to slope upward at a slight gradient, and presently I came to areas of the blackened earth that had previously glowed with fire. Then soon I found myself walking through billows of smoke and steam, between myriad fissures in the ground, which bubbled and glowed as though filled with molten lava, but now the stench in my nostrils grew ever more nauseating and I bethought myself to be within a land of confoundment and unreason

After a while I noted movement amongst a mass of soot covered rocks and continuing nearer this location I beheld black salamanders crawling amid the stones. The size of dogs; they basked in the heat thrown by the fissures of flame and wallowed in the pools of boiling rock. So it was with much curiosity I stopped to look closely within a pool near to me, and then truly did I grow sickened and appalled, wishing myself far away from this direful place. For within it I saw many glowing embers of broken human bone, smashed skulls, and a continual lurid bubbling of blood. Bathing in all this lay a huge salamander, its secreted toxins burning and withering away at the flesh and bones found within that poisoned mere. With this came the realisation that the foul and loathsome stench filling my nostrils was that of burning flesh. And now my proximity to the fire salamander was such that I was able to discern the black and red star markings along its back and see its empty, lifeless eyes, which paid me no heed at all. Other salamanders I also passed close to, basking in their pools and feasting on the melting flesh and bone, and though I held my scimitar in readiness, not one of them did show me hostility or even any awareness of my passing. So I endeavoured to walk swiftly through this landscape of terror, averting my eyes from the disgusting pools that bubbled and boiled about me.

Now, in some short while I chanced to come very near to the last grouping of stunted trees, and I was so filled with morbid curiosity that I strode up and took the thin branches of one in my hand to examine it. But upon exerting pressure upon the end of the branch, it snapped cleanly in my hand. Then came the dreadful understanding of death springing from death, for I saw that each 'tree' was in truth composed of twisted, blackened bone -- then I realised it was a surety that no soul within this awful realm could ever find eternal peace.

So I walked on as the gradient grew ever steeper, but still I dare not rest until I came to an area that could afford me some manner of concealment. But my determination gave me strength to overcome my weariness, for I had witnessed the fate Zhariman had in store for all mankind and so was resolute in my mind that I would fight against the evil of his Dark Way until my very last breath was taken!

Then my thoughts turned to the fate of poor Zareena, and at once my heart was flooded with anguish.

I stopped then, to make a brief observation of the inhospitable landscape, seeking an area of possible seclusion, and then I knew a sudden thrill of fear, for in the glow of the erupting fissures, I saw contrasted against the flame the slow movement of many dark, shrouded figures. Straightway I focused upon them more intently and noted that within their deathly grip they clasped the naked white bodies of what used to be men and women; doubtless doomed souls who were soon to know the flames of everlasting torture. And as this notion came to me, each struggling figure was then released from cruel, skeletal fingers to fall swiftly down into the deep fissures of raging fire and eternal torment. The still air of the Night Eternal was horribly rent with their agonised death-cries: the awful howling of alive-in-death corpses never to be blessed by the oblivion of true death.

In the following moments, there exploded from those horrendous pits and rifts, six columns of fire that scorched away the darkness like the baleful breath of demons angry with Heaven. At this, I crouched low and unmoving close the ground, my hand upon my sword, for I feared the eyes of Zhariman's dead servants might notice my outline in the glare of the brilliant flames. But this fear of mine proved to be unfounded, for now I saw that each shrouded form knelt with arms outstretched towards the fire-columns as if in spiritual supplication. Turning my eyes to find the cause of their sudden attention, I shuddered deeply, for within each column a fresh outline of vivid green flame gave life to an image of sublime evil: the image of Zhariman, the Demon Lord!

* * *

As the columns of fire again died down, I saw the slow movement of the Dead Ones as they returned once more to the concealing darkness of the Night Eternal. With this, I carefully recommenced the remainder of my ascent, but I now noticed that the ground beneath my feet was formed of broken lumps of charcoal and small gritstone rocks, and for the first time I wondered as to the possibility of any type of vegetation thriving within this region. For truly, I had seen not one sign of food or water, and this greatly troubled me, since I knew this realm had not been designed for one of life -- and the dead do not eat!

By now I had come to the end of my ascent, and pausing once more for observation, I became greatly amazed when I peered through the darkness across to the opposite side of the valley -- for there I saw, high upon an escarpment, a marvellous pavilion that blazed with living flame. I knew then a mixture of confusion and hope, for though the strangeness of the sight filled me with much awe and fear there was something about the *way* the pavilion burned which I disliked.

So I walked along the ridge, with frigid air continually biting at my skin, and the darkness ever seeming to press closer about me. And at this time the strangeness within my mind was something no man or woman will ever come near to knowing, for I walked within a realm forbidden to any of life, with only and always the stench of corruption in my nostrils, and ever a thousand lurking horrors seeming to watch me from the darkness of all eternity. The strangeness, the utter isolation and fear I felt as I walked through the solitude of that darksome place was something no man dwelling in sunshine and light can hope to experience.

Now, it was as I was walking along, encased within this solemn reverie, that once again the blackness of the void above gave way to that mocking image of Baul's own moon, but this time I refused to give acknowledgement to such a blasphemy, keeping my eyes firmly fixed upon the way I was to take across the scarp.

Though after some while, it seemed to me the white glow above had dimmed somewhat, and only some short time later I became disturbed by a sudden splash of liquid that fell to my hand. With a sudden burst of hope I made to examine the fluid, for the presence of rain would indicate plant life and mayhap a respite from my raging hunger and thirst, but the dimness of light allowed me no thorough inspection. With this I licked the droplet from my hand, meaning to taste its purity -- then I spat in disgust to the blackened earth! And looking up to the void above, I saw there a newly crimson moon which somehow sensed my outrage, for a torrent of fresh red drops appeared to fall directly from it, swiftly painting my face to mingle with the salt of my own desperate tears.

* * *

The cold wind eventually dried my bloodied face and stained clothing: the moon above once more reverting to the purest of white. And from far below in the gloomy valley came the distant sighings of wind through the tortured trees. So I paused in my walking, gazing down into the valley, and I saw that the ground was teeming with a multitude of death-black shadows. I noted also that the trees had now thinned greatly in population, providing no means for the uncertain moonlight to throw so many shadows from such emaciated trunks and branches.

At this, I recollected the time of my childhood when Khostrau had often delighted myself and Zareena with the telling of his *Tales of Night Eternal*, and always we had known many of his stories to be derived from the

Shah Nurmal, thus adding extra chills to our spines from the possible telling of truths. Then there came to me a remembrance of one certain night when Khostrau had told us of Yarna, The Valley of the Shadows. How we had marvelled at his thrilling tale of Zal, the Hero passing through a valley of black, featureless forms! But as these thoughts ran through my head, I suddenly became startled to see stealthy movements upon the valley floor.

At this I was filled with much fear and excitement, for it seemed the images created so long ago in my imagination, had now been gifted the power to come to visual life. Then, even as I watched, there came creeping into the valley a pallid figure of death in all its nakedness. This human moved slowly, upon all fours, at times reminding me of a dog in great fear of his master. Then I wondered to myself if this strange mode of movement was taken in way of stealth, or perhaps resultant from the cold and rigid muscles of death.

Suddenly I became aware that one shadow had slyly broken away from the others, and was discreetly nearing the naked form without his knowledge. With this, I gripped my sword hilt consumed with a longing to scream out a warning through all the darkness of the night and rush to the unfortunate's aid, but I knew to do so would undoubtedly bring about my own doom, for what use is a blade of steel against formless shadows? And what use delivering one whom was already dead? Then I saw the blackness of the shadow spread over the white skin of that crawling form -- and yet still it seemed unaware of the draining of its strength and soul. But it was soon after this the movement of the human came to an end, and instantly a multitude of tattered shadows rapidly closed about it like black vampires hungry for the inner soul. And the constant silence in which all this took place was dreadful and unholy, for not one scream was heard from that lifeless victim... as though hope had never been a part of its beatless heart.

When once more I continued on my way, I looked back through all the darkness of the valley to see again the flames of that pavilion which blazed with fire. But even at this distance it seemed strange to see how the flames licked about the walls -- as though in a loving caress. And then I knew this house to be Atesh Yarnath, The Pavilion of Mystical Flame.

* * *

I had no way of guessing the length of my sojourn, only that it had of a surety been a very great length of time, for now fatigue and hunger threatened to overwhelm me. But still I staggered onward, for nowhere had I discovered any place of safety in which to take my rest. After perhaps another parasang I finally perceived a rocky outcrop in the near distance, and with this sight, there did come a fresh vigour and force of will unto me, for I hoped this would be an area where I could shelter.

Presently I arrived at the outcropping and found it to be an area of large gritstone rocks. Looking about me, I soon found a cleft amongst the boulders that would afford me decent protection from prying corpse-eyes and the biting cold of the moaning wind. So I crawled into the cleft and then truly I gave way to my immense fatigue, falling immediately to sleep, despite my hunger. But during this time of rest, I was tormented by many visions of terror and nightmare, for it was a fact that although my body now rested, still my mind was haunted by all the dread things I had witnessed since my entry into this dark realm.

After some hours of fitful slumber, I regained awareness convinced that some deathly presence in the dark was now very near to me and had by some means awakened me. Though if this warning came to me from external sound, or by some other means within my mind, I cannot truly say.

So silently I rose up from the blackened earth, slowly moving out from the cleft that had given me shelter. And above, the moon seemed to be observing all, its beams falling to create shadows around the larger rocks, and it was amongst these shadowed rocks that I first saw *her*: A Drujs, gaunt and naked, crouched near to the earth and busily going about some unseen task with her cold, bony hands.

Stealthily I approached, forever trying to see the nature of her work, but as I drew nearer I saw the creature press her face to the ground and begin to snuffle at the earth as does a hound scenting its quarry. Now, the possibility of the dead breathing in the foul stench of the air had never occurred to me, for surely this was a notion never to be considered, even by the most crazed hashish smoker or opium eater. Then I thought of the Healing that Al Pharazeme himself had undergone, how on the very eve of his death his cold shell had regained the use of speech and hearing; and also of his doctrine that death was not truly the end of all. And with this I was given to wondering if this whitened corpse before me held other abilities.

So in a low voice I spoke a wary greeting, and immediately that ashen face turned itself in my direction

-- and from the brutal mouth came a sound of sinister hissing. Then, with movement of surprising speed, she was on her feet and loping warily towards me, forever sniffing at the stagnant air as though trying to catch my scent. And with this I stood solidly, sword drawn, legs apart and waited. Then, as the creature drew cautiously nearer I shuddered at the abhorrent vision of her face, for her whitened orbs were vacant, her teeth razor sharp and serrated like a shark, and her cruel mouth was bruised and stained with blood.

Still I stood my ground, but as the creature approached she paused, regarding me with her dead eyes. Then with a sibilant hiss she again turned and made her way swiftly back to the shadows of the rocks, and as I sheathed my sword with shaking hand I watched in silence as she bent to pick up some object concealed by the dark. With this she began to crawl away, soon descending through the scattered boulders on the side of the mountain like some leprous spider bathed in the light of the rotting moon. With the creature's departure I was taken by immense curiosity, and so started to walk over to the rock where I had first observed her, to perchance discover what object it was she craved there.

I knelt within the shadows, and felt along the blackened ground with my hands, not knowing what I expected to find, and ever aware of danger. But as I ventured further along, I suddenly felt the touch of something cold and soft that protruded from the dark earth. With puzzlement I took hold of the unknown object, tearing it free from the blackened soil. Then I made my way once more into the cold glow of the moonlight and there I proceeded to make an inspection of my find.

Now, the object I held looked to be a large black berry, though this observation would be due only to its shape, for truly its size was more akin to that of a pomegranate. But as I looked upon it I experienced a sharp pang of hunger as I wondered what strange fruit I had plucked from the blackened earth. This sudden craving was such that, without a second thought I raised the fruit up to my lips and bit hungrily through the outer skin 'till there came a sudden flowing of the inner juices -- and with this I grew sickened. For instantly I knew the taste of the 'juice' was that of human blood, and suddenly I realised my teeth had bitten through the charred remnants of human skin. So I cast the fruit aside in intense loathing and disgust, but still my raging hunger made me long for the bitter taste and sustenance it could offer.

As I again continued my journey into the eternal dark, I tried to turn my thoughts away from the biting hunger pangs which ravaged me, for I knew now the only surcease lay in those horrendous Berries of Death, which the *Shah Nurmal* names as Jazur Berries.

* * *

After I had walked along for a distance, which I estimated to be of no more than two parasangs, there came to my notice, by way of the moon's glowing, that the valley below me had now reached its end. I now looked upon the crumbling face of a mountain, tall as Mount Kaf of legend: standing in the sinister silence, it seemed a place more hostile and forbidding than any I had so far looked upon. A smooth track wound its way upwards, eventually entering into the darkened mouth of a cave; but as I stood observing this strange sight, a sudden column of scorching fire roared up into the night ahead of me, its raging sound shattering the eerie silence.

Framed against the fierce glow, I saw a darkly outlined procession of shrouded forms making their way up the winding track. Upon their shoulders they bore the weight of an ebony sarcophagus. But as I watched this macabre parade, there came another sound, sudden and dreadful, emanating from within the darkness of the cave. It was a voice of pure evil, a howl of darkness and hatred; a haunting scream of defiance to all that is blessed. And to my ears came pain beyond all description; to my soul a chill like Death itself. My eyes seemed to focus unwillingly upon that column of flame, and as before, I saw the image of Zhariman portrayed in vivid green fire -- but now the features were gloating and hateful, with a smile of intense cruelty and blackest venom.

Chapter V
The Pavilion of Sunrise

When thou risest in the eastern horizon of heaven
    Thou fillest all Perushia with thy splendour.
When thou settest in the western horizon of heaven
    The world is in darkness like the dead.

Prayer to the Sun - The Book of Shamash

FORCING MYSELF TO walk, I somehow dragged my eyes away from that visage of supreme evil. But now I looked upon the Dead Ones as they carried their macabre burden within the cavern. Other shrouded forms walked slowly back and forth like rotting sentries of evil, and I shuddered at the sight of those Undead Guardians of the Dark Way.

Then my mind began to fill with all the horrors of eternity, so that a billion tortured screams echoed in my head while mankind shrieked as one, and from my eyes flowed countless tears of grief, for always I thought of Perushia and the seeping twilight enveloping Sharador. Then through tear stained eyes I saw the distorted vision of those decaying sentries, and now they seemed nearer, much nearer, snatching at my soul, somehow magnified through my salted tears -- and I made to depart.

Then came a voice, perhaps the oldest voice any man could ever in an eternity hear, taking me onward to the very brink of madness; it spoke soothingly and with sly enticement; whispering with the sweetness of a seductive Peri; the scented breath of spring and the silent rapture of sunrise. Yet always it contrived to tempt me towards that cave of darkness -- but I refused to comply, for I would never submit to that direful Dark Way, for this was Uruk-atil, The Cave From Where The Dead Ones Walk, and I wished to be away.

* * *

For some time I walked across the desolate landscape passing the mighty peak until in the distance I descried a slender, arched bridge that spanned a great chasm. My soul was gripped in the clutches of a great fear then, for this structure was known to me. It could be naught but Zinvat, the bridge that spans the fathomless chasm Sindroo.

As I drew nearer the bridge I saw that it was fashioned from the blackened bone of humans and was scarce an arm's length wide with no handrail for balance or safety and I bethought me that Gorannon, the Skull-lit Bridge of Evil was but a pale imitation of this mighty span. As I stood at the chasm's brink and looked down I discerned far below me roiling mists and vapours, and within these billows I glimpsed pale forms writhing in the cloudy depths, their faces distorted in anguish. Faintly I could hear their desperate cries and oft times it seemed that they called to me, pleading with me to turn back and abandon my quest. Such suffering eclipsed anything I had seen thus far, for I knew these to be souls doomed to eternal torment in the white mists of Sindroo. These vapours stripped the flesh from the bones of their victims, causing them to twist in agonising torment as they were slowly and subtly divested of their meat. This torture lasted aeons, after which the naked frames, blackened by the consuming mists of Sindroo, were added to the construction of Zinvat. Above all they were creatures to be pitied, for their pain was exquisite cruelty and their torments ever subtle.

As I gazed into the gulf, tears of sorrow staining my cheeks, I heard a mellifluous voice behind me:

"Greetings Khalik, I have been awaiting you."

I turned and beheld a redoubtable Jinni. He stood thrice my height and had skin of crimson hue, great black, bat-like wings, twisted horns, wicked fangs and evil amber eyes. He was clad in purple dyed pantaloons of tanned human hide and human skulls hung from a rope slung about his brawny neck.

I knew utter dejection then, for of a surety, my doom was sealed: before me stood Yindra, the Demon. Ceaselessly he guarded the bridge and chasm and it was written in the *Shah Nurmal* that he would lie concealed beneath the bridge and that he would cast any who dared attempt to cross it into Sindroo's fathomless gulf. Had my quest, only newly begun, come to an end?

Yindra spoke again:

"What no words of greeting for Yindra, Mighty Hero? Have thou nothing to say before I cast thee into the depths of Sindroo, there to endure eternal torment?"

I drew my scimitar, planted my feet firmly part and faced the terrible Jinni.

"Stand aside, Yindra, for I would cross!"

The demon smiled, and I saw with horror that each of his yellowed fangs was almost as long and as wickedly curved as my trusted sword.

"Such bravery! Indeed thou are a Mighty Hero! Or, perchance a mighty fool!"

I stood firm while the demon mocked me.

"Fear not pitiful creature, for it is not thy destiny to know the torments of Sindroo. Know this, gnat upon my backside: Zhariman has put a geas upon me that I let thee cross my bridge, for He is awaiting thee. But know this foolhardy adventurer, I did dream a dream which concerneth thee and thy quest to slay the Demon. In this dream I did behold thee upon the golden roof of the royal palace. There you did espy a company of bizarre demons who did cavort and caper most mysteriously. Asking them of them their intent they replied to thee that they sought camels. To this thou replied in astonishment: 'What, camels upon roof-tops?' Quoth they in answer: 'And yet thou seekest to slay Zhariman'."

In truth this was a cautionary tale for those who would be cautioned, but I would not be turned aside from my quest by the sly tongue of a Jinni, despite having a very lively dread. Yindra stood aside and mockingly bowed low gesturing for me to cross the bridge. With much trepidation, for I feared a cunning trap and expected Yindra to seek to push me into the abyss, I walked out upon the slender span of bone and looking neither downwards nor behind me crossed slowly, sword in hand, to the farther side of the mighty chasm.

Now there was no return for me lest I slay Zhariman, for Yindra would of a surety not let me cross a second time, and, his geas fulfilled, would not hesitate in hurling me into Sindroo's awful depths.

*   *   *

After I had traversed several parasangs beyond that dreadful place, travelling a desolation of scarps and crags, there seemed to rise up from the ground wreaths of ethereal mist. A sepulchral silence encompassed all, and it seemed as though I passed through a mausoleum of darkness whose silent occupants grieved for victims of some immense transgression or tragedy. But always I walked with great awareness of evil, for I knew no part of this direful realm could be judged as safe, and always deceit and danger would strive to claim me for I knew this realm to be the mist shrouded Plains of Rudah.

Now, it was after some time spent in walking through these mists of perpetual quietude, that there came to my eyes a very curious sight, for the mist of one particular area was lit with orange luminosity. And so I stood for a while, hesitating, and ever thinking it could be some sinister trap or unknown peril that I looked upon, while about me the fumes twisted in strange curls which suggested copulating demons. But still the curiosity in me was such that I slowly grew nearer that mysterious glow, and as I did so I wondered if perhaps madness had truly claimed me. For in one instant the mist rapidly lifted and revealed a strangely shaped pavilion of burnished gold and amber and bronze.

I gazed upon that strange structure with incredulity and utter amazement, for its very existence seemed contrary to everything I had witnessed in this evil realm. The glow I had experienced radiated from the building itself, its brightness appearing to purposely defy the misty dark. But all that building was rounded; and with no definitive roof or sidewalls, it gave the illusion of a miniature sun rising from the earth.

Still I approached this peculiar spectacle with great caution, ever ready to draw my blade, for I realised the mist had lifted only when I had hesitated in my progress -- as though it tried to lure me with colour and a promise of warmth. But as I grew nearer, a vague sound reached my ears; it was a sound that seemed strangely alien to this unholy nightmare realm -- for it was the sound of the sea.

Now I realised that this place was girt round by water and was approached from but one direction while the ground beyond the pavilion fell away sharply to reveal the sight of breakers pounding on rocks far below. The sea looked grey and cold in the light of the counterfeit moon, just a melancholy expanse; in areas it was mist-wreathed with grotesque shapes twisting slowly upwards. Then the sudden thought came to me that perhaps Gandarewa, the water demon, had gone insane and sculpted these ethereal forms from his coral palace beneath the waves. And the sheer terror of this thought made me turn back to face the peculiar pavilion at my side.

Stepping into the glow of the shining walls, I was able to see the vague outline of a door. I hesitated for but a second before reaching out to touch it, and was filled with a sudden dread when, on an instant it swung inwards. But still I entered within, and there I found a brightly lit chamber with every bevelled wall containing scenes of sunrise, each tapestry cunningly shaped to meet the curvature. The floor was paved with black marble filigreed with ambergris and the ceiling painted in the richest of yellow pigments and figured with gold and bronze.

In contrast to this there stood a gaunt figure shrouded in folds of night-black satin. He seemed unaware of my presence, and went on silently studying the tapestry he stood before. On his hollowed, angular face was an expression of perfect rapture, and it seemed to me he was taking in every detail of the depiction, revelling in sheer delight. Suddenly he turned and walked towards me, speaking with a disconcerting voice, for his tongue it dripped honey and his words were as poisoned sweetmeats to the unwary.

"Welcome Khalik to Shamash, the Pavilion of Sunrise! I am Changra Bel, the Man of Visions."

A bright orange circular image, surrounded by flame was emblazoned on the front of the shroud he wore; the sigil of Surya, God of the Blazing Sun, a startling contrast against the black. He reached out a fleshless, taloned hand to shake mine, but at the touch he recoiled, face distorted with obvious shock.

"But... You are warm... One of the Heartbeats! How can one of the Heartbeats ever leave Jilyah?"

I spoke slowly and clearly in an effort to keep the anxiety from showing in my voice, and stared directly in his eyes.

"I have passed through Shotu, the Tunnel of Darkness from the realm of Life, and my purpose here is to destroy Zhariman. What is this Jilyah for I saw no mention of it within the *Shah Nurmal*?"

A sly smile slowly spread across the ashen features of Changra Bel's face, his whitened tongue licking over thin, mean lips.

"You are indeed a rarity. And I must say you have been most fortunate to stumble upon the safety of my humble abode. If you have never heard of Jilyah, then I will tell you of it. It is a vile place; a place in which the Heartbeats are confined and allowed to breed -- a constant supply of food for the Dead Ones!"

With this disclosure I was shocked: shocked to find that Khostrau had been wrong in his assumption that I would be the first owner of heartbeat and soul to enter this dreadful nightmare realm. Then suddenly there came to me the sound of the outer door closing softly behind me, but still I tried to prevent any apprehension from showing upon my face.

"How long has this harvesting of humans been going on?" I asked.

"Since time out of mind," he replied. "All this place is evil, with only the Heartbeats showing any measure of love for each other. But I too, you can trust and rely on, for once I also lost my heart to a girl."

"I am astounded Khostrau did not know of these things." I spoke my thought aloud.

"Khostrau? Khostrau you say? Then we have a mutual friend. For many years we have corresponded, Khostrau and I; with our magical skills we kept in contact, our thoughts and visions silently passing between our two realms. Why, Khostrau would on occasion send me wondrous works of art the which to decorate my abode, so of course I did not taint his mind with words of Jilyah. But how know you of Khostrau?"

"I was his friend," I replied sorrowfully.

"Was? Then..."

"Khostrau is no more: a victim of Zhariman."

"Ah, so the wheel turns. You are welcome in my house, for any companion of Khostrau's is indeed a friend of mine!"

There was something about Changra Bel that I did not care for, a curious half-suppressed gloating expression lurking within his indigo eyes that made me uneasy. It seemed to me he was purposely neglecting to mention his own role in this dark scheme of things.

"I am also here in search of a girl called Zareena -- perhaps you have seen her?" I asked.

He stared at me in calculating fashion, seeming to carefully choose the words of his reply.

"I have never met this girl, but I have heard it said she frequents Jilyah. There she is known as Sister Midnight. It is a dangerous place for one such as you, but if you are adamant upon going, first you must partake of food and rest to restore your depleted energy -- or your quickened death will be inevitable."

When I nodded my agreement, he led me through curtains of dyed black cotton into the chamber beyond.

* * *

Each wall of the room we entered was painted turquoise, and the centre of the floor was taken up by a bright orange orb placed upon a tripod of ebony, which actually seemed to emit golden rays of sunlight. A sudden thrill of trepidation ran through me when my eyes settled upon two cushions and a low table carved from whitened bone. I saw dark shadows drifting across the carpets but could see no objects by which they may have been cast. Then a vague sound of whispering reached my ears. Slowly a shadow moved across the floor towards me, arms rising above its head to display shadowed hands with taloned fingernails. Changra Bel raised his own hands, at once causing the singular form to retreat and merge with other shadows which thronged and moved with a curious disquiet.

"They cannot cause you hurt while you dwell within my abode, though they may perchance try to frighten you -- *they are my pets!* But enough talk, for you must be ravaged with hunger."

At these words Changra Bel motioned with his hand towards the table, and I saw with surprise that this time its surface was arrayed with bowls fashioned from the bleached skulls of marmalukes, each containing the loathsome Jazur Berries. And though I felt repulsed, my sudden craving for sustenance was such that I knew I must partake of this unwholesome food. So we walked over and seated ourselves upon the cushions, then I watched as Changra Bel began to feast upon the berries like a hunger-ravaged animal, his whitened tongue now stained with red as it licked about his mouth like a questing parasite. Then I too, reached into one of the bowls and began to eat; I commenced to devour the fruit in the same nauseating fashion, for sheer hunger had now overcome any scruples within me. And as we ate, I saw countless shadows constantly flickering over Changra Bel's body -- as though in utter adoration.

When our repast was complete, Changra Bel proffered me a bowl of water and I washed my hands. Then he lifted his cushion and placed it beside my own, so that we both faced the direction of the central orb. He turned to look in my face, and deep within his indigo eyes I glimpsed utter insanity.

"The time approaches when Surya will rise up into these dark and desolate skies; the blood of the Dead Ones will quicken, and the essence of Life will thrive within this forsaken realm. For I tell you that on one occasion my eyes witnessed that great orb of fire show itself briefly above the sombre horizon. Look now into the Inner Orb and you shall observe that which my eyes once gazed upon."

With this, I saw his face begin to crease with mental exertion, and instantly my sight was pulled involuntary onto and into the orb: it began to draw my vision, my very spirit within it. I then looked back, far back into the cold, dark history of this Death Realm, and to my eyes came many scenes of suffering; while filling my ears were plaintive sighings and laments -- corpses wept tears of blood at memories of their loved ones.

Then there came to me a sense of floating high up in the frigid darkness of the Night Eternal, travelling back through fathomless ages, while far below I saw the shrouded forms of the Dead Ones knelt in supplication before those dire columns of flame. Then I grew astounded at a distant sight, for even in these dim, past ages Atesh Yarnath burnt with constant flames of frenzy. And this vision brought to me a terrible feeling of awe and unease, for now I knew Atesh Yarnath to be cursed most mightily.

Through ebon skies I travelled, and beneath me came into view Uruk-atil, The Cave from Where the Dead Ones Walk. And it was with this vision that I grew more fearful, for even though it was my spiritual being which travelled above that baleful place, still the Dead Ones grew aware of its presence. Their cadaverous faces lifted to the skies and their unholy vision pierced the very ages! Then, swift as thought, I returned to the Plains of Rudah, which once again were mist-shrouded. But soon I saw the orange glow of Shamash, the Pavilion of Sunrise, and here my spirit hovered and seemed to wait.

After some time, the mist dissipated, lifting so quickly that I gazed in awe at the spectacle it afforded, for all the nearby cliff-top was lined with shrouded dead. Their tattered, decaying skin flapped in the demon winds like the blown cloaks of enchanters. They gazed out over the grey ocean, and in their midst I saw Changra Bel. In the following seconds, I too, was afforded a sight of the heaving sea, and a feeling of great wonderment grew within me, for in the eastern skies the black horizon was staining deep red with a blossoming which slowly extended into searching fingers of orange flame.

And as I watched in awe the sun rose up majestically into the Night Eternal!

For fleeting moments this dark realm was transformed into a world of bright sunlight, untold abominations cowered and scuttled in the searing light, seeking shadows and darkness - then came a sound unholy beyond all imagination. A voice of deep thunder howled through the aether and shook the very ground with the magnitude of its force. It was the terrible voice of the Death Realm itself! The air darkened and thundered and the earth trembled and quaked. There was a mighty roar as though the heavens were falling upon the earth and the sea swelled wild and threatening. The waters grew suddenly frenzied, bubbling as though seething with sheer anger; the angry wind whipping the surface like the flails of tormenting demons. Then the voice of thunder raged again, this time more intense and prolonged, and in the skies above came an explosion akin to the beginning of the universe itself. Then swiftly this world of death fell once more to utter darkness and the sun was extinguished.

* * *

Again I was travelling through the mists of ages and time flew like a moment enchanted. A whirl of visions and incidents flowed before my eyes and my mind reeled before infinite vistas of pain and suffering. But something amongst all these scenes of torture and distress I viewed caught my attention: for I saw the image of my beloved Zareena entering the Pavilion of Sunrise, and Changra Bel standing there to greet her. Then to me came a shock greater still, for I was given a brief but perfect view of Changra Bel's face -- and I saw it was not whitened at that time, or dead, but healthy and alive.

* * *

Suddenly I knew intense pain and my eyes filled with an incredible brightness. In the next moment I found myself seated once more beside Changra Bel bathed in the uncanny light emanating from the Inner Orb and surrounded by shifting shadows. We sat for a while in silence, and when finally I turned my gaze upon Changra Bel I saw his colourless cheeks were stained with crimson tears.

"You see, Surya *did* once rise." He spoke like a child proving his infantile point.

"Yes, I now see things with more clarity," I replied, but my words referred to the image of Zareena and the fact I had been lied to. Then I dearly wished to look once more within the Inner Orb.

The Man of Visions stood and walked to the centre of a wall, touching it with the palm of his hand, causing a concealed door to swing inward.

"Come, I will show you to your sleeping chamber, for it is now night in the House of Changra Bel and you need sleep!" With these words I knew for a surety that insanity had fully claimed him.

I followed him through the door. The chamber we entered was decorated in a mixture of deep blue, white, and orange; the carpets, hangings and floor tiles giving the illusion of clouds floating high up in a warm summer sky, tinted by the light of the sun. But truly I was exhausted, and so I was grateful, even to a madman, for supplying me with a chamber of such opulence and comfort in which to slumber.

For some while Changra Bel lingered in the doorway, his eyes full of silent jest.

"Sleep long, my friend, sleep long. For the Night Eternal has no sun to warm your bones; has no-one to bless the tears you will shed, and no rest to give you when you are dead."

And truly the words he spoke disturbed me so much that I wished there was some manner in which I could secure the door, but this seemed most unlikely, for as he closed it, it became merged with the wall and was invisible to my eyes. Yet my fatigue was such that I collapsed gratefully onto the bed of cushions and rugs. It was then, as my eyes grew heavy with sleep, that there came a gentle decline in the light from that artificial sunrise and, as I succumbed to exhausted slumber, the room filled instantly with the enveloping darkness of the Death Realm.

Then my haunted mind became gripped in the talons of nightmare and my thoughts strayed to recently vacated tombs, strewn with cracked bones and discarded sarcophagi; lids gnawed through and scratched and shattered by the vengeful dead. And in my sleep I tasted the stale and vitiated air upon my tongue; heard the cries of the Daevas on the wind, and looked upon the image of Zhariman portrayed in dancing tongues of green flame.

My nightmare unfolded, presenting to me the vision of Al Pharazeme's manic face smiling with sensual satisfaction as he copulated with three Jinnyah. Then I saw he drained the life-blood from the throat of one of these willing females, and at this, I screamed with shock from a revelation of ultimate horror, for as she smiled a lascivious and lustful smile, her face became my own!

I awoke, frenzied and sweating, back in that room of utter darkness. But there was a sharp pain in the side of my neck, which corresponded to the memory of my nightmare, and something warm - something warm and wet that trickled down my skin. A dim glow of sunrise began to emanate from the walls, responding to my returning wakefulness, and in these seconds I heard a sound of shuffling upon the floor. Then I beheld the dark outline of a figure scuttling, scorpion-like towards the hidden door.

Suddenly everything became lucid and a raging anger coursed through my veins. I leapt up from the bed, throwing myself in the direction of Changra Bel with all my strength, for that dark, crawling figure was indeed he, and though the creature now had the door half open, still I managed to pull him back, throwing his body savagely to the floor. His pallid face gleamed in the artificial sunrise, his crimson lips smeared with fresh blood that I knew to be my own.

"Foul vampire! Unclean demon! Tell me, what have you done with Zareena and where is thy master, Zhariman?"

He remained silent, and once more that familiar gloating expression returned to his cadaverous features. But by now my rage had taken full possession of me and I slammed his head forcibly against the floor again, again and yet again!

"I am numb, I am cold," he spoke quietly, "do what you will, you cannot cause me harm. I will tell you only that Zhariman is currently at his most vulnerable, and that Zareena is far from the helpless creature you seem to think she is."

And hearing his words, I knew that he spoke the truth and that a mere mortal such as I knew nothing about inflicting pain on one beyond death. So I brought my fist down heavily on his cold face and his head immediately slumped to one side, eyes shut. My anger melted for I was satisfied that at least I had taken the consciousness from him. So I stood and walked to the area where I knew the concealed door to be and searched the wall with my fingers, for once more it had closed. My hand eventually found that which it sought, the raised carved head of a coiled viper. I pressed upon this once and the door swung open. When I turned to look again at Changra Bel, I saw his head had already turned to face my direction; cold eyes studied me intently as I left the room.

So it was that I descended the steps and passed through the door into the room of the Inner Orb. With this, there came to my ears a sudden sound of puzzled whispering and myriad shadows closed swiftly around me. But knowing they could do me no harm, I walked purposely over them, instantly inciting their rage. Then I seated myself upon a cushion facing the Inner Orb, my eyes fixing intently upon its glow, and I focused all the mental energy of my spiritual being towards entering the stored visions of Lost Ages.

Then came the deathly chill of the Night Eternal as darkness again enveloped me.

* * *

Once more I was travelling far above the ground, past events and places unfolding below me. But this time I saw my own self travelling through Shotu, the Tunnel of Darkness. Using all the willpower of my inner being, I found that I could make certain changes; Time became my plaything as I searched the hidden folds of history. Then I saw majestic palaces of frozen darkness, and strange, stunted forms of death; all twisted with agonies of torture and pleading for the release they could never know; I saw figures of flame with bubbling tears that fed their own pain and I saw distorted bodies encased in ice, their eyes filled with frozen tears -- while walking through corridors of coldest cruelty was a dreadful Entity of the Darkness, face set with savage satisfaction. And at times Azmaraz, the Angel of Silence touched my ethereal ears in appalling mood, so that I craved for a sigh from the lonely wind. But when, at last, the single sob of a saddened corpse filled the void of sound, it sounded to me like all the planets of the universe had collided in a maelstrom of destruction.

On this occasion I saw other dark forms travelling far above the moonlit ground and with a deep shudder recognised the Dead Ones; lines of them travelled in upright rows moving silently through the cold air of night, cerements flapping like the wings of carrion crows. And with this I grew greatly afraid lest they should turn their dull, rotting orbs skywards and discover my helpless spirit. But they seemed more concerned with their own malign mission, so vaguely I wondered what destination these servants of Zhariman sought. And I saw that they passed straight over The Valley of the Shadows, then onwards, high above the mist-vapours of the melancholy ocean.

Soon I came to the Plains of Rudah whose mists conceal The Pavilion of Sunrise, and indeed I saw the glow of orange walls far below me. With this, I began to pray with all my being for another vision of the occasion when Zareena had entered this bizarre abode. And truly my power of thought must have grown very much greater by then, for it seemed but only a matter of seconds and this very scene was granted me. Then I prayed that I could learn the fate of Zareena within that strange abode, and immediately the exterior of the pavilion became transparent and in a strange manner unknown to me, also magnified the events that transpired inside.

Then I watched helpless while Zareena mutely admired those tapestries of sunrise, and I saw the taint of sadness touch her face when she recognised scenes that also hung in the palace of Al Pharazeme, her father, and I saw Changra Bel constantly talking to her. Oh how I did ache to reach out and touch my love, to take her in my arms and whisper sweet words of comfort. But Time and Space were barriers to my desires. Then I saw the familiar look of repressed anger upon Zareena's face, and I knew she grew tired and insulted by the constant discourse - so I thought that it must be a vile trick of Zhariman's when I beheld my beloved embracing Changra Bel; lingering to seductively kiss his cold lips.

Later I saw their naked forms supine upon scattered cushions, and it seemed almost that they lay upon a sunlit cloud within a deep-blue sky. But I felt sickened when I saw their bodies entwine in the act of copulation. It was a violent union and my heart shattered as I watched. Then I discerned Zareena's fingers; tipped with black talons, dig deep into the flesh of Changra Bel's chest. And truly, if a spirit could have laughed mine would have done so, for in the next moment I realised the identity of the girl to whom the Man of Visions had lost his heart!

Suddenly I grew concerned, for I saw the brightness of the watching moon was becoming quickly absorbed. I had spent too long within the lost realms of the Inner Orb. I determined to make haste to return, for I did not wish to be caught in my current spiritual state, and misplaced in Time by some cunning trick devised by Changra Bel. So I turned from those vistas of times gone by, moving back towards my physical being with all haste through Time and Space. But on my journey I observed with mounting dread the constant darkening of the opal moon, and when at last my spirit burst outwards from that Orb of visions past, it did so lit by only the merest glimmer of pale moonlight.

Pain racked my body as once more I found myself upon the silk cushions, while filling my ears were a thousand angry howls of disappointment. And in looking once more at the Inner Orb, I saw its entire surface was covered with swirling shadows, except for one small area of neglect. Then I understood that those dark forms had attempted to imprison me within the Orb, and with this, I was consumed with vicious fury at their sly scheme. So it was that almost without thinking I strode over to the dim-lit Orb, and smashed my sword hilt violently into the midst of the shadows. Immediately there came a sound of splintering as the Orb burst into a million fragments and the room fell to utter darkness.

Then I heard many cries of anger and frustration, accompanied by the sound of hurried footsteps descending the stairs without the chamber. So I moved through the darkness, feeling the touch of decaying draperies as I passed into the next chamber, but this I found to be also shrouded in darkness. And so I began to run my hand over the outer wall, searching for the mechanism to open the door, which would give me exit once more into the Night Eternal. But when I eventually located it I found the door opened only very slowly, almost as though unwilling to allow me egress. Stepping outside finally, I looked back to see the orange glow of all the outer walls was rapidly fading, and with this I realised that the Inner Orb must have been the source of power for all the pavilion.

Then I walked a short distance and crouched low in the darkness, for though I knew it was a foolish thing to remain within this area, still the fires of curiosity burnt bright within me. And just before the glow of the pavilion flickered for a final time and was extinguished, I looked back and saw the outer door forced open for someone to emerge. This dark form then walked along the top of the cliffs, occasionally looking down with eyes that searched. Then the moonlight caught Changra Bel's gaunt face, and I watched as he began to move swiftly in the direction of Zinvat and the cave of Uruk-atil.

Chapter VI
The Sea of Sadness

The whispering wind rolls in off the waves,
Weeping with the voices of the lost and the damned.

The Shah Nurmal, Book III

FOR SOME DISTANCE I walked beside the cliff-top above the waves. My mind was in a greatly shaken state, and the deathly chill of the vile air permeated my body. But soon I perceived that the cliffs were now becoming less sheer. Then in the light of the baleful moon I saw a narrow path had been worn into the blackened ground. It was most puzzling to me as to why there should be a regular ascent and descent by this way, for below I saw only the melancholy sea and a broad, sweeping beach of ebon sand. So with my curiosity growing ever keener, I decided to descend by this route to the shore below.

As I made my way downwards, I studied the sight of the solemn sea, and once more I viewed those grotesque, twisting wreaths of mist that seemed to emerge from beneath the surface of the water. Then suddenly I stood and listened, for mixed with the strange sough and moan of the sea-breeze and the distant crash of breakers, I heard something disturbing beyond all I had so far known, for a sound of weeping travelled from the sea itself. Gently filling my ears came the saddened cries of souls borne on the wind, each whispering voice telling of untold sorrow and endless suffering.

At that, I looked once more upon the grotesque images of mist coiling above the waters and a tear of pity stained my cheek. It was at this moment I knew these waters to be Vouruskasha, The Sea of Sadness.

Reaching the end of my descent, I stepped onto the blackened beach and began to walk toward the waves that lapped its shore. In doing this I noticed the soft texture of the sand beneath my feet, its dust-like nature being as light as ash. And truly, the strangeness of this awful realm was now such that, of a surety, no one could have ever experienced the like even in the throes of an opium delirium.

The intensity of the cruel moon suddenly increased, and beneath the surface of the sea I beheld whitened forms that fought in frantic effort *not* to rise up to the surface. But their struggles were in vain and always their solid forms would break through the surface of the water and dissolve into the air, forever forming those bizarre misty shapes.

In the following seconds I was shocked and appalled to see all the mist-shrouded areas of the ocean erupt into vivid flame. Then filling the air came countless screams of agony as the souls of the dead began to rise from the sea and burn. Such was the intensity of this awful resonance I was forced to cover my ears with my hands in an effort to silence the terrible cries of torment. They burned with a thousand hues and shades, and with mounting horror I saw each burning form begin to move towards the shore I stood upon. I ran down the dark coast in sheer panic, for what use was a blade of steel against forms of living flame? Yet still occasional burning entities came to rest near to me -- as though the ebon sands somehow entranced them.

* * *

Only when every flame had died into the dark of the eternal night and every soul was destroyed, did I slow my headlong pace and make an examination of my immediate surroundings. About me I found many piles of the ash-like sand. Then a chill of dreadful realisation ran through me, for I knew the entire coastline to be formed from the charred remnants of human souls. Thereafter, with every step I took I shuddered at the thought of each poor spirit, alive-in-death, beneath my feet. And though I prayed to Zallah and the Seven Gods that all had finally found blessed release, still a morbid certainty grew in me that it was not so.

Now, in some while I saw that my peregrinations had brought me near a small bay, covered with white stones and large pebbles, which shone as brightly as a concubine's ambitions in contrast to the blackened sand. But as I grew nearer this area, I became appalled to see I looked not upon pebbles or stones, but at shattered bones and crushed skulls that littered the ground. And after walking some way further, I came upon a skeletal body that was almost complete, save that the skull was half buried and parts of the femur appeared to display signs of having been gnawed. Perhaps at this time I had become touched by too much loneliness, for suddenly I was taken with the foolish desire to look upon its face -- even if that face were of salt-washed bone.

So I worked eagerly with my hands, brushing away the black sand from the visage, and eventually I was able to hold the skull up to my own countenance. Then I voiced my thoughts in soft whispers, telling how good it was to look upon a human face (though I did not mention the lack of flesh); and I spoke of the earth; of the sun and of warm breezes; of fields, forests, and flowers, and the blue skies and seas and of all the wonders of Perushia. But always I was careful to give no mention of Zhariman, or of the darkness currently encroaching upon the world. Then something happened which caused me to cast the skull away in revulsion -- for from the empty sockets of the eyes trickled tears of black blood.

Suddenly an unaccountable anger gripped me.

"A thousand curses upon you!" I screamed, "perhaps the truth may cheer you instead, for Perushia is now dying; enshrouded in darkness and lost to the vile will Zhariman."

In the following seconds I became deeply ashamed of myself as I realised I had been stealthily touched by a spirit of despair, malignity and desolation: a victim of the oppressive evil abroad in the Night Eternal.

* * *

I had walked a distance of perhaps a parasang along the black sands leaving the Bay of Bones behind me, when I noticed an opening in the rock at the base of the cliffs. A beam of silver light fell from the moon to clearly illuminate the mouth of a cave, and with this I grew very wary, for perhaps the sickly orb sought only to lead me into danger. So, reaching the cavern mouth, I cautiously advanced within, the blade of my drawn sword reflecting the moon's rays.

Reaching a point beyond which the light could not penetrate I stopped, sheathed my blade and sat with my back against the smooth rock wall, intending to rest for but a moment. But the rhythm of the waves and the soothing darkness contrived to lull me...

* * *

I awoke to find myself shrouded in the velvet darkness, and there came to me then the sound of waves echoing within the depths of the cave. With this, my first choice of action would have been to run blindly back out into the dark, and, of a surety, this is what I would have done had it not been for a sudden sound of sobbing. Now, perhaps the sheltering walls around me had deflected the malign contamination of the Night Eternal for the sounds of sadness I listened to caused me only great distress and sorrowful emotion, so that after some seconds I spoke into the dark:

"A blessing upon you stranger, if you can understand me. Is there some way I can be of aid?"

Immediately there came a muffled cry of shock from the rear of the cave, as though someone who had previously been unaware of my existence was now cognizant of my presence. After a slight pause there came a voice; a voice which seemed something like Al Pharazeme's in its quality; unused in centuries and as cold as Death itself, and yet... wary.

"I am beyond aid now, my friend, if friend you be, for it is much too late. All I seek now is quiet and solitude -- but mayhap you have come to end even those last pleasures?"

The voice was such that I could not decide whether it came from a young or old man, yet there was something about it (a sense of honesty and hopelessness) that touched me greatly.

"I promise I mean you no harm," I said. "I am but a slave of this atrocious realm, caught within its black web and yet fighting for all the world. For Perushia is even now becoming shrouded in darkness, being drained of light and life by the venomous will of Zhariman, and only I, with heart and soul intact, can end this crime against humanity by bringing about his death."

Now I seemed to see something that stood amongst the darkness, a vague figure, featureless, no more than a shadow but discernible by a deeper quality of black -- as though Ulasto Vidath, the Harvester of Souls stood before me!

"My blessing upon thee stranger, for your motives are pure and good, and by comparison my own fate is deserved the more so -- for I have sought the knowledge of the Dark Way, and now I pay the price."

"Then you have my sympathy," I replied, "for one of my own blood may soon be seized by the Dark Way through the corruption of her mind."

"Do not seek to ease my conscience," said the voice, "for my own mind was already corrupt... but perhaps I may yet achieve redemption and pray that Zallah's eyes will see into even this damnable world of death."

"Perchance the only crime you committed was one of curiosity," I said, "like a moth drawn to the lamp, you did not realise the full peril and consequences until it was too late -- the penalty you are paying is cruel and unjust."

I saw a vague movement through the darkness of the cave, and a chill came over me as though something long dead now stood very near.

"I wish you could look upon my features," said the voice, "maybe touch my hand in friendship... but all I can offer you is a breath that will freeze your very soul. There is nothing to fear in the darkness of this cave. You must move through it and ascend to higher levels, for if you stay here the sea will surely claim you as one more accursed soul."

And so it was that I stood and without another word began to walk carefully to the rear of the cave, my hands continually touching the wall for support and bearings. Then after some while, I began to climb upwards over what I judged to be boulders and loose shale, which eventually led me to a cleft. Here the voice in the darkness spoke once more:

"Here you may rest."

And presently, as the waves flooded into the cave, meaning to drown me, we laughed together while they crashed in impotent anger far beneath us. But soon the deathly voice grew serious once more, and many were the bizarre things it did relate.

Then I grew appalled to hear how the Dead Ones regularly descended the cliffs by way of the path I had taken, always obscenely eager to cull salt-preserved flesh from the Sea of Sadness.

After a spell of silence, I began to tell of my encounter with Changra Bel, and how I had destroyed the Inner Orb.

"You must leave this place," said the cold voice beside me, "for the Man of Visions can never be trusted. Already he will have informed the Dead Ones of your possible whereabouts, and when the tide retreats they will come to search this place."

"Then where must I go?"

Suddenly his voice sounded distant, no more than an eerie whisper.

"Walk deeper into darkness and you will see."

Now, I knew a great doubt about following the advice given by the voice in the darkness, but at length it came to me that I had no other option. So it was, that I began to stumble like a blind man, my arms held outwards before me, and ever thinking I was about to walk into some contrivance of greatest evil. But as I continued in my slow progress, it came to my notice that the stone floor I walked upon had now grown very smooth and was beginning to form a downward slope. At that, there came to me the dreadful thought that I was now descending into the black heart of the Death Realm itself.

In a short while I perceived a faint eerie glow in the gloom beyond which caused me to pause in fearful doubt. Then it was that, as I stood in silent observation, I realised that the greenish glow was emanating from the rock walls of the cavern tunnel in which I stood. So, warily, I continued on my way, and the luminosity of the walls grew steadily brighter the further I walked. With this, I was able to walk faster and with more ease in my mind, for any obstacle would now be plainly seen and thus less of a danger to me.

With the light of the walls, I was able to discern that I not only travelled at a slight downward gradient, but also that the tunnel was beginning to turn at a very great angle. I became very puzzled by this, for it seemed to me that by now I could only be heading back in the direction of the sea.

Some short while later a curious sound came to my ears. It had about it the quality of a deadened roar, as though some fearsome creature of the Night Eternal had grown aware of my presence, and that somewhere far above me it roared in futile rage. And all the time I walked, there came a steady increase in that awful bellowing noise above, until eventually, I began to fancy I felt actual vibrations within the tunnel. Very soon my progress became halted by an abrupt dead-end.

My ears were assailed by a cacophony of thunderous sound, while the way ahead appeared to be sealed by a black wall, which blocked the entire tunnel. So in curiosity I walked towards this obstacle, meaning to see if any possible way beyond it could be gained. And as I walked nearer, I saw the centre of the wall contained the upright lid of a tomb. At this morbid sight I became curious, placing my hand upon the surface to feel its texture. With this, I became amazed when it slowly opened at my touch.

Immediately the thunderous roar grew in volume a thousand-fold, and looking ahead I discerned the cause, for I saw the awesome sight of the deep ocean roaring all about me, only to be deflected by something invisible to my eyes. So I walked within that chaotic cauldron of sound, turning suddenly, hand on sword hilt, when I heard the oblong entranceway close behind me. Quickly I looked about me, and came to realise the astounding fact that I now stood *within* The Sea of Sadness. Reaching out before me was a long crystalline corridor, which somehow withstood all the roaring pressure of the thrashing sea. A peculiar lambent glow filtered through the air, dimly lighting the way forward. So, after observing my immediate surroundings and perceiving no obvious threat, I at once began my careful progress along the corridor, for there was no telling what may lurk within these bizarre confines, and perhaps I had already stumbled into some trap of frightful evil.

As I walked, my hand ever upon the hilt of my sword, the thought came to me that this macabre passage could only have been built by the Dead Ones to enable them to gain access beneath these tear-salted waves. But by what means they achieved this I pondered without success. Then, as I made a slow but steady progress, there came a gradual dimming of the light in the corridor, though in contrast the depths of the sea began to fill with a greenish glow. And it was in this jade light that I began to see visions, which could only have been plucked from the nightmare mind of Shaizan, the Evil One, himself. For within the sea existed the sallow faces of many sorrowful corpses, each one fighting a cruel will which meant to raise them to the surface. Then I saw the sight of pallid, skeletal bodies, every one chained by their ankles to the bed of the sea, and I prayed that nothing more than underwater currents caused their occasional movements...

As I walked I gazed out at the tormented souls within the Sea of Sadness, knowing that the tears constantly flowing from the eyes of each woeful form contributed to these melancholy waters. Soon I grew greatly ashamed and wished only that I had some place to conceal myself, for I sensed they had peered deep within my own soul, growing very saddened by something they had witnessed there. Then I knew for a surety they had in somewise gained knowledge of my devouring their own flesh and blood, almost as though the stains from the Jazur Berries still smeared my lips. Soon, each dead face drew near the transparent sides of the corridor, and then, in one instant, every sorrowful expression turned to that of intense hatred; pale lips mouthed cruel words of rage. With this I could withstand no more, and so ran hastily into the further dimness of the corridor.

* * *

In time I had outdistanced the weeping corpses so I slowed my headlong rush, for I had entered an area of pitch-blackness; darkness reigned both in the sea and in the passageway. I now made progress slowly and with extreme caution, ever aware of possible danger. And at all times as I walked, I continually touched the side of the transparent tunnel, thereby gaining my stability and exact bearings. It was but a short time later when a stray shaft of light played across the floor and came to rest at my feet.

Constantly this slim beam of light would flicker and point: a spiteful finger of denunciation -- or perhaps one that beckoned? And like the most foolish of moths, the light drew me onwards. Soon I came to stand before a forbidding black door that blocked the corridor. It stood slightly ajar, outlined by a crack of light.

Peering into the room beyond, I saw it to be filled by a hazy yellow mist, which, it seemed to me, purposely concealed anything contained within. But still I entered inside, sword in hand, for, of a surety, this place could offer nothing worse than the horrors I had already looked upon, and perhaps it may even afford a brief respite, for I was near exhaustion.

As I entered, I became paralysed with fear, for the mist swiftly evaporated and a doom-spell held all in its grip. Central to the room there rested an open sarcophagus, inside which reposed the figure of a young woman, exquisite even in death. Around the edge of the tomb were six black candles of corpse fat, each recently lit and affixed to bone-carved holders. In the opposite wall was a corresponding door to that by which I had entered; it also stood ajar. So I sheathed my sword and walked up to the sarcophagus, my breath frosting visibly in the candlelight and myriad shivers travelling down my spine.

Inside there lay a female figure. I saw her dark eyes were open, wide and beautifully defiant, yet in them was a chill to freeze the very sun. Her naked skin; pale perfection; alabaster white, played host to a frenzy of flickering shadows and it seemed they danced wildly in delicious celebration of death. I lowered my face toward hers, for though I knew her dead eyes were unseeing, still I had the strangest desire to gaze into them. And truly it would be no crime for me to kiss one such as this, even in death? But when my lips so very lightly touched her frozen cheek, I became appalled, for in an instant the delicate features of her face became those of my own visage!

Outside the room I heard the sea taken by a sudden rage, pounding on the outer walls like the Death Drums of the Drujs. And in the candlelight I saw that once again the lambent mist was forming. It hung above the face of the cadaver, (which now bore my own countenance!) like a gaudy yellow mask. Slowly the cloud descended to obscure the body and in that very instant every candle was extinguished simultaneously. Then the room fell to an abrupt and preternatural silence; even the angry sea ceased its turmoil. And now I became trapped in the void of quiet for the stillness of the room had enveloped my mind. Then, for a second my mind teetered on the brink of insanity, for it seemed that my soul peered from the dead eyes of the cadaver, and with this came a knowledge that no other mortal had ever possessed: I experienced the knowledge of Death itself! And it spoke to me of the silence between the stars; the sheer nothingness of a teardrop in the ocean, and just when I thought all had been said, it spoke of the stupidity of love, and the madness of devotion.

Then I was once again within my own mortal shell. I staggered away from the tomb and groping my way through the gloom sought the door I had noticed upon entering this Tomb of Death. As I pushed my way through the door a voice emanated from the direction of the coffin, and I screamed when I recognised the voice was my own:

"None can escape their Destiny!"

* * *

Again I walked slowly onwards through the oppressive darkness of the passageway, and slowly there rose within me a very great anger and determination. I wondered if I had been shown my approaching fate, and if the Night Eternal would eventually claim me body and soul. Then I realised that this experience was yet another attempt to break my will and to portray the hopelessness of pursuing the Demon. But the thought came to me:

what does the fate of one-man matter if he can free the world of a dark grip that means to choke all its life? And with this thought I walked on with renewed determination, for I meant to rescue Zareena and destroy the evil of Zhariman even if it meant the destruction of my own soul!

Now, as I walked through the gloom, there came to me a feeling of great unease as though something malign lurked nearby in the dark. As I walked onwards, this feeling began to slowly heighten, so I walked most warily and with my eyes continually peering into the blackness of the corridor ahead.

I had travelled a measureless distance without discerning anything of concern when suddenly there came a loud knock on the underside of the transparent floor I walked upon. Motionless, I stood and listened, wondering if some dire creature of the sea had somehow detected my passing. For some moments I remained thus, standing immobile and in complete silence, in the hope that whatever was outside would now depart.

As there was no repeat of the sound I again continued on my way, though I did so very slowly and quietly, for it was my intention not to betray my whereabouts. But it was after only a short distance when there again came a loud knock upon the passageway beneath my feet, this time of such force that I felt the tunnel vibrate about me. This caused me great concern, for were the tunnel to crack, the relentless ocean would consume me. I looked down at the area beneath my feet and it seemed to me that a vague white shape showed indistinctly through the transparency. Uneasily I wondered what manner of creature it might be that could so easily keep a track of my movements, and I reassured myself there would be very little chance of it breaking through a structure that could stand all the immense pressure of the pounding sea.

I got down to my knees and lowered my face to the floor, meaning to make a much greater inspection of this unknown creature. But as I did so the entire passageway about me became illuminated by a bright white light that revealed the sallow bodies of many corpses pressing against the exterior of the crystal the corridor. The unquiet dead had found me again! But then I knew a very great pity as well as shock, for I realised I looked upon those foolish enough to attempt suicide in The Sea of Sadness. I was disturbed to see every blanched face was turned towards me, and the look on each countenance was that of utter insanity!

It was at this time I grew sickened by a frightful understanding, for of a sudden realisation came to me that these corpses within the Sea of Sorrow were nothing more than vile provender for the flesh-hungry Dead Ones.

Looking down, I saw many forms with dire expressions of anger and hatred upon their decaying, bloated faces, pounding their fists upon the crystal in a mad impotent frenzy. At this, I began to hasten, for now I envisaged a time when my own sanity would also be absorbed into the black heart of the Night Eternal, and this thought held the greatest fear of all for me. But as I ran rapidly across the floor, every section of the crystal corridor flooded with bright light at the touch of my sandals, and with the light came always the hollow pounding, so that soon the entire corridor began to tremble with the insane violence of the undead. I ran onward and, as I felt the tunnel beginning to rise, began to look desperately for the end of the passageway.

Chapter VII
The Image of the Torturer

Death harbours in his languid eye
And slays with every glance
He pulls the strings that bind your souls
And watches as they dance

Zal in the Land of Demons

EVENTUALLY I CAME to an area of corridor that ceased to glow at the touch of my feet, and just a short distance further I felt the ground grow soft. Soon there came a chill breeze upon my face, and with it came that awful miasmal stench which permeates this entire sickening realm. In a short while the malign moon thought to show itself through blackened, scudding clouds, and with its glow I found myself to be walking along a shore of dark sand and what I took to be shingle.

I had escaped the unquiet dead of the Sea of Sadness!

Some way ahead I saw the vague outline of sheer, overhanging cliffs, and winding upwards, a set of stone steps that appeared to be hewn into the black rock. As I studied this stairway carefully, I saw two shrouded forms slowly ascending. For a brief moment they stopped in their climb, their faces of yellowed bone gleaming in the moonlight as they turned to gaze out over the solemn sea.

In the following seconds I was filled with an intense dread, for the mouth of one baleful form opened, and forth into the night came a howl such as the storm demon Azi Dahaka made when it was consumed in the river of fire, Ayohsust. Following this I froze in a stance of total fear, the terrible silence broken only by the sound of the breaking surf. And truly, there could have been no greater illustration of the black heart and soul of evil contained within that form of death than its direful voice.

Then I beheld a darkened form walking along the sands of the beach towards the stairway, so I hastily moved myself into the deep shadows cast by the towering cliffs, crouching low behind fallen rocks to avoid detection. Then it seemed to me that the moon became filled with vile anger, for it seemed to throw its illuminating beams beneath the over-hanging cliffs in an attempt to draw me to the attention of those malign corpse-eyes. Great was my relief when that dark figure passed by unaware of my proximity.

After some while I stepped out from my place of concealment, and looking up to the stone steps, saw that all three Dead Ones were now ascending together. And so for some while I rested in the shadow of the cliffs, thereby affording them sufficient time to complete their ascent, and when I deemed it prudent I made to continue on my way.

When I reached the steps, I began my own ascent very warily, ever aware of my surroundings and of any possible danger that may be lurking, for the many bizarre things I had already seen and heard within this realm of death were of a surety only a very small part of what might lie concealed in the enshrouding dark. And as I climbed upwards, I heard the wind sighing; a sorrowful breeze which spoke of all the melancholy souls imprisoned in this place of endless suffering; then I heard the gentle soundings of the surf, as though a million tears spilled from the saddened surface of the sea. But now I only laughed darkly to myself, for no longer did I trust the deceiving elements of this detestable realm!

Now, when I eventually reached the top of the stairway, I looked all about me with keen eyes in order to ensure my immediate safety. With this, I saw that all the ground was burnt and charred, continually smouldering as though forever about to erupt into scorching fields of fire. And the smoke that rose from the ground troubled me greatly, for it had about it a sulphurous quality that stung my eyes painfully and made breathing most difficult. But the smoke also brought another, far greater danger, for it now made it difficult to observe my surroundings with any degree of clarity. So I began to walk slowly over the blackened ground. But now my way became arduous, for above me the smoke had almost obscured the watching moon, and though I felt some pleasure from escaping the scrutiny of that hateful orb, still I very much missed the illumination it had so gloatingly sent down upon these nightmare adventurings of mine.

After some further space of time spent in walking, I heard a series of distant screams causing a knot of fear within my vitals. At this, I screwed up my eyes and attempted to peer through the shadowy smoke. Then there came to my ears a tremendous roar of sound, soon followed by more screaming. But this time there was such an agony contained within the shrieking that I covered my ears with my hands to gain a blessed respite. Following this, I saw briefly through the smoke, that large areas of land about me had violently erupted into bright orange flame. And yet, before my eyes could clearly take in all the detail of that distant scene, there came a thicker cloud of sulphurous vapour that rose up from the ground to swiftly confound my vision. But still in that same direction I maintained my footsteps, for such was the human quality of pain within those beseeching screams, I would have gladly risked my own life if there had been any way to halt the suffering.

Now, the amount of time it took for me to arrive at those blazing areas of flame came as some indication of the agony and volume of the cries of the sufferers. For truly their screams had carried a very great distance to me. Though at last I came to stand beside the nearest fiery inferno and truly did I wish to avert my eyes from the horrific sight I beheld then. For there I saw the charred remnants of many humans, their blackened bodies tied to upright stakes thrust deep within the ground. Then I grew most truly sickened when the stench of their burning flesh assailed me. With this, I wanted only to be away; far away from this place of loathsome atrocities, for I had remembered the words of a certain tale spun for me by Khostrau when in my youth, and I realised I was now gazing upon the Fields of Atesh Ghah.

So I began to walk rapidly through a small area free of fire that ran between the fields, but now the moans of those trapped in eternal torture filled my ears once more. And perhaps it was the fact the field to my left had almost ceased burning, which caused me to be foolish enough to glance inwards at the nearest charred occupant. For with loathing I saw the remains of that revolting figure upon the stake lift its blackened head towards me. The dark, blistered skin of the lips opened for a groan of incredible suffering to pass forth, followed by heavy sobs and distorted words that begged only for release. But when I began to turn away, unable to withstand such a sight of sickening torture, I saw the man's mouth stretch wide and begin to scream imploringly into the dark of the Night Eternal.

* * *

Now, I had passed rapidly by two more fields of scorching fire, when I saw something moving slowly through the flames to my right. The figure was cloaked in sable raiment and moved steadily through the shimmering heat and constant blaze as though totally unaffected. Occasionally it would stop beside a screeching form impaled upon a stake, carefully lifting the charred face upwards and staring almost tenderly into the burnt, agonised features. And often that gaunt form would halt in its progress, head tilting upwards as though savouring the stench of burning meat that filled all the air. But in one instant my heart was filled with utter despair, for that cruel visage in the centre of the field suddenly turned in my direction. I stood, unable to move; for I saw those pale lips form into a smile of appalling evil. With this I grew most afraid, for I remembered Khostrau's stories of old, and my readings of the *Shah Nurmal* and so knew the figure observing me was that of Akomar, the Torturer.

Without any hesitation his dark image began to stride purposely towards me, his face twisted with a deep loathing. And though I tried to turn and flee along the path between the Fields of Atesh Ghah, perhaps I may have been held by some spell of puissant evil, for not a muscle could I move to help myself. Then, as Akomar took the final few steps toward to me, it seemed my very soul began to suffer from the evil of his near presence, for suddenly I became encompassed by a fusion of scolding heat and icy death-chill. In the following seconds I screamed with agony and unparalleled shock as the malignant image of the Torturer strode right through my body.

From somewhere behind me there came the sudden sound of rancorous laughter as I collapsed to the ground, but turning my head, I was amazed to see the form of Akomar continue walking into the opposing field of flame. With this I knew a mixture puzzlement and relief, for at that moment I had felt it was indeed a surety that my soul was to be ripped from my body. But while I continued to watch the black form of the Torturer, I saw his body begin to shimmer and fade to eventual nothingness. With this, I knew that I had looked only upon a magical *projection*, a creation of Akomar's evil sorcery, and that Akomar had used vast stores of magical energy in order to physically touch his victims at a great distance.

For some seconds I remained seated upon that blackened pathway between the Fields of Atesh Ghah, for though the horrendous sights and sounds around me were almost unbearable, still the harrowing experience I had just undergone had drained me greatly of physical and mental strength.

But after a while I made to get to my feet, for the possibility suddenly came to me that Akomar would, even at this moment, be regaining his own strength, so that I did not dare stay for too long in one position and risk the return of that dread image.

So for some while I walked rapidly upon the small path leading through the Fields of Atash Ghah, and I was most relieved when there came an eventual end to those unholy fires. And so I made further progress through the Night Eternal, coming at last to a place where I could no longer hear those horrendous screams of human suffering. But always there would remain a great sorrow and anger in me, for etched into my mind was the disturbing thought of what it must be like to scream for all eternity.

* * *

I had walked a very great distance beyond the Fields of Atash Ghah, when there suddenly came an ominous sound that seemed to reverberate throughout all the realm of the Night Eternal. It had about it a regularity that I found vaguely familiar but could not place, almost as though a thousand men with hammers pounded in unison upon the blackened earth. The barren landscape around me amplified this sound greatly, and also it may have been that my ears had grown much more sensitive to any noise, such was the silent nature of the void I walked in.

At this time I became aware that the treasonous moon once more observed my progress, occasionally peering down slyly through gaps in the scudding clouds. To my surprise its beams suddenly broke through the heavy clouds to illuminate my dismal surroundings in far greater detail than ever before. With this, I saw a range of black hills, which stood perhaps a parasang away. And though I found it most suspicious that the moon had highlighted these hills to me, still I had but little option in my choice of way, for in every other direction I saw only a black emptiness.

So I continued in my walking towards those sinister-looking hills, but with every step of the way there came an increase in the sound of the strange hammering.

When I eventually came near the black hills, I saw that there were occasional gritstone boulders and rocks upon the slope. With further observation I noticed that a single path had been worn into the scorched earth and with this I grew very cautious in my movements, for I realised that there was the possibility this was but another route taken by the loathsome Dead Ones in their service of the Dark Way. So it was that I chose to ascend the hills by a route of my own choosing, for to take a defined pathway would be risking danger of discovery. And so I moved up the hills very stealthily and all the while the peculiar hammer-like sound of thudding grew ever louder in my ears. But it was as I reached the halfway point in my ascent that I came to walk very near to a rocky outcrop of boulders. With this, I must admit that I was taken by a very great curiosity and also *hunger*, for part of the nearest boulder hung over the darkened earth to create a deep shadow of blackness.

So I looked about me, until I grew assured that I was in no imminent danger. Following this, I got to my knees and began to search with my hands in the shaded area of the boulder, almost immediately coming across a grouping of Jazur Berries. Then for some while did I stay beside that boulder to gain my sustenance. And all the time I ate, I offered silent prayers to Zallah and the Seven Gods for those unfortunate ones whose misfortune afforded me this food, and then I swore that I would avenge their suffering.

When I had eaten a sufficiency, I continued my ascent of the hill. Now that my hunger and thirst had once more been sated to a certain degree, I felt stronger and determined that all my energy should be given to opposing Zhariman's Dark Way. But still the pulsing sound of that rhythmic thudding filled the vile air, increasing in volume all the while I made my progress, so that I became desperate to reach the highest point of the hill and see if I could determine its cause.

When at last I came to stand atop those darksome hills, I stood aghast at the sight I was then afforded. For beneath me lay the strangest village I had ever beheld, with many low buildings outlined by the guileful moon, as though it sought to show plainly my destination. As I gazed upon this uncanny sight I realised that I looked upon Jilyah, the Village of Heartbeats. Perchance my mind was now becoming attuned to this realm of evil darkness, for as this realisation struck me there came a sudden cessation of the thudding sound I had been subject to for so long.

Chapter VIII
Jilyah

Sister Midnight, Sister Midnight,
Dances in the crimson moonlight,
Craving blood all through the long night,
Walks upright when she has no right.
She's your curse is Sister Midnight.

The Songs of Jhal, Volume XVI

NOW, PERHAPS IT was the supernatural properties of this place, or perchance the constant silence which reigned throughout all the Night Eternal, but by some mystical means I had somehow been gifted with the ability to perceive the beating hearts of those humans residing in Jilyah. It came to me then that this uncanny sound I had suffered had been only *a representation of life* heard within my mind, for with the sudden discovery of its origin, it had faded most rapidly. Then the thought came to me that perhaps the Night Eternal had teased and tortured me with these sounds of trapped humanity.

So I stood there for some while, silently observing the sight of the Village. And with this I noticed that not one human form walked those sombre streets. And I saw that all the buildings of Jilyah were domed or oblong-shaped, standing very sinister in the moonlit dark. A chill of great fear ran through me as I remembered that every Heartbeat residing within the Village was nothing more than food for the Dead Ones! But I also recalled the words of Changra Bel, and if it be true that Zareena, known here as Sister Midnight, really did frequent this place, then I was determined that I would find her at whatever cost, staining my blade with crimson gore if needs be. So very slowly and cautiously I began to descend the opposing side of the black hills, my eyes hard with grim intent.

But as I strode down the blackened ground towards my destination, I happened to glance to my left and was able to see that the worn path I had so carefully avoided also descended in the direction of Jilyah. Unease grew within me then, for this suggested that the Dead Ones made regular use of this way, and their sickening purpose I already knew too well. After some time, my descent came to an end without any untoward happening, but still the deathly silence brooded and no sign of life within the Village was visible. And perhaps this served only to heighten the sense of foreboding within me, for if I had seen but one Heartbeat walking freely, then maybe I would have hurried and been in haste to talk to them.

Now, after some while I came to walk the deserted streets of Jilyah, and I was able to make a closer inspection of the buildings about me. Yet always was I filled with a sense of dread for I saw many of the oblong-shaped buildings were in the manner of large tombs and mausoleums, each one windowless and silent. And with great apprehension I approached the building nearest to me, for curiosity now compelled me to make a more thorough examination of it. But what I saw filled me only with repulsion and shock via the macabre revelation that all the building was constructed of blackened bones. This reminded me once again of the unrivalled cruelty that was abroad throughout the entirety of this dreadful realm.

Then there came a noise to my ears. Peering through the gloom of the street to the building directly opposite, I saw a door begin to slowly open. And though fearful of what I may see, still I kept my eyes fixed upon it, but all the time my hand remained tightly clasped upon my sword hilt. Then suddenly there came the sound of a lowered voice and these words I heard:

"Brother Heartbeat, pray come in from the street before the Dead Ones find you, for at this very moment they are within the dwelling next to you."

But I knew not whether to trust these whispered words, for already I knew much of the cunning evil within this dread realm, and all I could see in the doorway was the vaguest outline of someone -- or some *thing*. In the following seconds however there came from within the house next to me a sudden scream, followed by the sound of pleading voices, and subsequent to this I heard a deep sobbing. And it was the sound of this heart-rending sobbing, I think, which gave me the resolve to cross to the house opposite, for it was a surety there was something of great cruelty taking place within those charnel walls.

So with cautious haste I crossed the narrow street, and beheld the vague figure of a man stood within the shadowed doorway. His raiment was all but rags, but still he appeared to be in health as good as my own, though within his eyes there was a look of deep sadness and concern, which touched me greatly. With alacrity he ushered me inside the building, closing the door immediately. Two candles stood in the centre of an unfurnished room and within their flickering shadows a woman and small girl sat shivering.

"You are new here, Brother Heartbeat," spoke the man. "Tell me, why do you come to this place of your own free will?"

"I have journeyed here from the realm of life, to bring death to the one known as Zhariman. But perhaps you may help me, for I am also here in search of one of my own kin, you may know her as Sister Midnight." And with these words of mine came a look of sudden fear and outrage upon the face of the Heartbeat.

"Please leave my dwelling. I do not wish to welcome one such as you within my home. For if you are in any way related to Sister Midnight, then it is apparent you are evil to your very soul!"

I became most angry at these words, and also at the vile insult he had aimed at my beloved Zareena.

"You call this a home? It is but no more than a large tomb!" I spoke these words with much venom.

"Then it is very appropriate," spoke the Heartbeat. "Perhaps if you were to look a little closer at my wife and child you will perceive the curse that Sister Midnight has brought upon us."

And truly, as I walked nearer the centre of the room and studied his wife and child by the uncertain candlelight, I became appalled to see their skin was pallid and bloodless. Then something further caught my notice; something that caused the deepest dread and horrible realisation in me, for I saw deep puncture marks upon the necks of each. This caused me to finger the scars upon my own neck, inflicted by Changra Bel's loathsome feeding. Their sad eyes gazed upon me and they shivered with a chill I knew would soon be eternal.

"They will dwell in a death that is not true death," said the Heartbeat.

"I am sorry," I replied, "I did not know."

Suddenly there came a great upheaval from the street outside. I walked over to the door, opening it just wide enough to gain a discreet view. Outside, I saw three of the Dead Ones dragging a man and woman from the house opposite. Both bled from a variety of wounds upon their naked flesh, while heavy chains led to leather collars closed tight around their throats.

"Where are they taking them?" I asked the Heartbeat.

"They will be made to walk to a place of eternal pain," he said. "The Fields of Atesh Ghah are the feeding grounds of the Night itself."

* * *

When I had given sufficient time for the Dead Ones to depart, I left the house of the Heartbeat, for I had grown shamed and shocked by Zareena's devotion to the Dark Way. Though still in my mind was the thought that she could be liberated from this curse of evil. After a while there came the sight of other Heartbeats cautiously emerging from their macabre houses, and often I would receive the greeting: "Live long, O Brother Heartbeat!"

Now, after I had walked some way, I began to leave the houses of the Heartbeats behind, instead walking through an area of the curious domed buildings. It was odd that each of these edifices seemed completely sealed, with no sign of any doors or windows, and though I pondered long on what these domes could hold, I had not even the vaguest idea. In a little, I approached a dome very much larger than its surrounding companions. Outside it there stood an emaciated Heartbeat who watched me curiously.

"You are new here, O Brother Heartbeat. May I humble myself before you and offer assistance?"

The Heartbeat bowed low and kissed the ground before me.

"I am sorely troubled," I replied, "I have heard it said that Sister Midnight is within Jilyah, and I do not want to feel her lips upon me."

"Your concerns are understandable," he said, "but there is naught to cause concern, for I have heard it said that Sister Midnight sleeps within Rahyani, the Perfumed Gardens of Death."

"The whereabouts of The Perfumed Gardens of Death are not known to me." I said.

"Truly O Brother Heartbeat, you do not wish to know what or where those gardens are. Be at ease and get pleasure from the time you have remaining."

There were three stone steps leading up to the dome, and these I strode up to stand beside the Heartbeat.

"What is this place?" I asked.

"This is the place of our entertainment," he replied, smiling warmly, "for it is the Pavilion of Pleasure and Pain."

A morbid curiosity grew in me; the urge to know what manner of entertainment was afforded the Heartbeats.

"Would it be possible for me to enter this place?"

"But there is currently no show, O Brother. Alazaar is not yet due to entertain us with his scenes of splendour and intrigue."

"Still, I would like to enter."

"Then do so, O Brother. But there will be little for you to see as yet, save maybe the preparations, and I caution you, if you would be cautioned, not to be there when Alazaar arrives."

Then the Heartbeat descended the steps and walked away into Jilyah, an expression of great puzzlement playing over his features.

* * *

As I turned and walked toward the doorway its doors parted slightly to allow my entrance as though instructed by a spell from the most powerful magus. Inside, I found myself within a gloomy corridor, lit only very dimly by wall-lamps spaced far apart. Walking slowly, I followed the passageway until I came to reach an archway decorated by candle-lit skulls, and sealing this was a large black door. Reaching out my hand toward the door I was much surprised when it opened silently at my merest touch.

Now, when I passed through the door, I was startled by what seemed to be a thousand peering eyes that filled a large void of darkness. Then for some moments I stood frozen in my stride for each one of those unblinking eyes was of a lambent green, and this, for some reason, suggested to my mind the presence of a great evil. For several moments I remained still, and presently my eyes became accustomed to the deep dark. Thus I eventually came to see the 'eyes' more clearly. Then it was that I quietly laughed to myself for I saw before me only a theatre full of seats, each with green emeralds placed within their arms. It was these that had caught the shifting light of the lamps and shone bright and hard as the eyes of demons to give easy identification in the gloom.

So I walked some way down the aisle I now stood in, until eventually I neared the dim-lit outline of a stage. And though the curtains currently appeared to be open, still, from what I could see, there was no sign of activity upon the platform. My intrigue was now very great, and so I made to sit on the chair nearest to me and ponder on many questions for some while. Perchance here I would learn of the location of the Perfumed Gardens of Death. But perhaps the strain of recent happenings had played greatly upon me, for in only a few minutes the dimness of the light had seduced me into a deep slumber.

* * *

I awoke abruptly; startled to wakefulness by a sudden sound, and for some seconds I struggled to recall my whereabouts. The time spent in sleep had dulled my senses somewhat, so there came to me a great feeling of vulnerability and unease. And so I sat very still and in silence, until such time as I could ascertain the cause of the sound that had awakened me. But in these seconds of silent waiting there again came to my ears more sudden and unexplained sounds, and this time it was clear to me that these noises were emanating from the direction of the stage. I could hear the dragging and clinking of metal, plus sudden dull thuds, as though heavy objects were being moved and placed in certain defined areas.

In time my sleep stained eyes had adapted to the extent that my immediate surroundings began to be revealed to me, and eventually it was apparent that a lone figure was manoeuvring objects about the stage. Then I recalled the words of the Heartbeat who had said I was likely to witness the preparations taking place for the next entertainment. With this, I became less uneasy, and realising the figure upon the stage had not yet become aware of my presence, I spoke out loudly to him:

"Does the entertainment commence presently?" I asked, but in reply I witnessed a sudden cry of astonishment and fear.

"I am sorry," said a strange, fearful voice, "it is indeed a rare occurrence to find one inside the theatre when entertainment is not in progress -- unless it be Alazaar and his slave, Jalur the demon!"

"Who is this Alazaar?" I asked. "How is it that just one man can inspire such fear in people?"

The reply I received from the Heartbeat chilled my heart.

"Alazaar is known by some as Akomar, the Torturer!"

For some seconds I remained stunned by the revelation. There was now complete silence as the figure stood unmoving in the dimness, then suddenly came the sound of a solitary sob, followed by the sound of clinking metal as the figure moved across the stage.

He spoke quietly, helplessly, while he walked: "You see, I am the one essential part of his act, mesmerised nightly to blank the horrendous knowledge of death from my mind, I am the subject of endless torment and scorn from the depraved audiences of Heartbeats, eventually experiencing the ultimate horror that I am no longer a man of life."

The sorrow within me was overwhelming; I became consumed with a desire to help in some manner. Leaving my seat, I ran towards the stage, stumbling up the five wooden steps and on to the bare floorboards. Now I was able to see a pale shell of a man walking slowly, restricted by cold muscles and the metal chain, which dragged awkwardly from his ankle, but still I was too late. From the far side of the stage came the creaking of a sepulchre opening.

"But surely there is something I can do...?" I spoke desperately.

"There is nothing," he replied. "But I may be of service to you."

"How so?" I said warily, for great was my mistrust of all within this treacherous realm.

"Sister Midnight sleeps within Rahyani, the Perfumed Gardens of Death. Seek her not and you shall find her." With these cryptic words he climbed into the tomb, chains scraping against the stone. "Please let me sleep now," returned his voice, "for know I can never truly die."

Chapter IX
The Perfumed Gardens of Death

> It is written that every soul must drain the cup of Death. For He is the Destroyer of all delights, the Sunderer of all societies, the Depopulator of palaces and the Garnerer for graves.
>
> *The Shah Nurmal, Book IX*

IN MY POSITION upon the stage, I was able to perceive many wicked instruments of torture and persecution and I knew a feeling of great unease. So I made haste to leave that place of vile 'entertainment', and continue my search for the Perfumed Gardens of Death. Walking onward through a barely visible doorway, which stood in an area of deep shadow at its very rear, I left the stage.

Just beyond the door I entered a narrow, sloping passageway, which was illuminated by dim, flickering lamps, the luminosity they afforded being singularly vague and indistinct. Yet still this meagre lighting was enough for me to discern odd markings scratched into the wall, and my curiosity was such that I made a closer inspection. And in examining an area directly beneath one of the lamps, I was able to determine that many deep scratches had been gouged into the brickwork. I then used my hands to examine darker areas, and in these places I also found evidence of deep scratches, each one running horizontally.

After a short time spent in walking, it came to me that there had been a gain in the air temperature, and I assumed this to be due to the gradual downward sloping of the corridor, my deduction being there would likely be more fire-pits and fissures of flame beneath ground level. Presently there came an ending to the flickering wall-lamps, yet still I played my hands over the surface of the narrow walls, all the time feeling the continual presence of those deep scratch marks.

Perhaps this curiosity of mine distracted me, for suddenly I found myself tumbling downwards into some unseen chasm. I seemed to be falling into a fathomless gulf, my screams echoing as though I descended into some vast vaulted cavern. Then my body plunged heavily into water. Momentarily I was stunned, and I found it difficult to orient myself in any manner, but with a mighty surge I broke through to the surface of the water and realised I had plunged into a subterranean lake. About the perimeter of this lake, but a spear's cast away, there was a huge causeway hewn from the living rock. Infrequent fire-torches were fixed to the walls of oozing stone, each burning in the dark like demonic eyes. The temperature of the water was agreeably warm, and that which I had inadvertently swallowed I found contained more salt than any sea I had ever known. In the glow of these fire-torches I saw that the surface of the water was beginning to bubble and it came to me that the temperature of the water was quickly rising.

Immediately I swam toward the edge of the lake and hauled myself up on to the causeway. Here I crouched for some minutes, resting in silence and taking in the sight of the lake. As I watched there was a rapid increase in the bubbling of the surface and I realised that the infernal waters were now boiling – I had pulled myself from the lake not a moment too soon. Then I perceived that something had floated to the surface of the pool adjacent to the part of the causeway on which I found myself. Peering through the gloom I saw it to be a body, and the soaked raiment it wore could not disguise the nauseous fact that it had begun to cook. In the following seconds I was aghast to see similar bodies rise to the surface. With this, I made haste along the gloomy causeway, for it was now obvious to me that the bodies of the lake were but weakened forms of death, and the Dead Ones appetite for human flesh was very well-known to me.

After skirting the lake for a little distance, I came to an area that allowed me a vague sight of many dim-lit passages, and in this direction I made my choice to walk, giving blessings to Zallah that some exit had been afforded from this dread place. But just some little distance before I reached the opening to the nearest passage, I heard the sound of a rhythmic, metallic, squeak from somewhere above. Looking up into the higher regions of the cavern, I saw that a large metal cage was slowly descending from a ledge upon a rusted chain, and within it stood one of the black-shrouded Dead Ones, an oil lamp clasped in a skeletal hand.

It was apparent to me that the cage was being lowered to allow collection of the boiled meat of those unfortunates within the lake, and I did not wish to remain and watch the gathering of their helpless bodies. So I entered rapidly into the nearest tunnel, and it came as a shock to me to find the only light to illuminate my way came in the form of an eerie glow emanating from the rock walls themselves. Also, in sharp contrast to the heat of the cavern, the air carried a deathly chill that increased the further I ventured.

* * *

I had walked for what seemed like many hours, though perhaps my judgement may have been distorted by the constant cold and fear of what may perchance lurk within the dark. Often, when I came upon junctions where other tunnels crossed my path, my ears would detect the sound of footsteps or the murmurings of things unholy. Yet still I walked, until after an uncertain length of time I began to crave the presence of light and a place of safety, for I had become very cold and greatly fatigued. So, I determined to stop for some short while, sitting with my back pressed against the cold stone wall, all the while listening as I scrutinised the dimness for any stealthy sign of approach. As I sat in reverie, I called to mind the tunnel, Shotu and Gorannon, the Skull-lit Bridge of Evil, and how those bizarre structures and their malign intelligences had somehow become aware of my presence.

* * *

After I had grown rested somewhat, I continued on my journey, and, at length, passing round a curvature of the way, I beheld a vague light that appeared to filter down from the roof of the tunnel. So it was that with much stealth I very slowly approached this emanation, all the while alert and prepared to turn and flee or fight at the slightest movement or sound. But upon my approach to this area, I was surprised to see that the roof gave way to a narrow stone staircase leading upwards, and somewhere far above, an unwholesome white light fell to display many worn, slime-covered steps.

Once more there came to me the nauseas charnel stench of the Everlasting Night, but this was now almost welcome to me. For these Caverns of Cruelty beneath the earth were contrived to stain the minds of any with morbid derangement. So I began a slow ascent of the stairway, the disgusting mould leaking slowly beneath my feet like the rotting organs of a decaying corpse. Occasional streaks of crimson formed a network of thin veins in this growth, as though the whole downward-flowing seeping mass had become one huge entity that slyly crept. Soon I found myself avoiding it unconsciously, for some far region of my mind warned me of a danger not yet fully apparent.

Yet in time I came safely to the top of the staircase. Once more my eyes looked upon the face of the malign moon, and I knew its beams had reached down to purposely guide my way. And with this I cursed, violently screaming at the fraudulent heavens and that counterfeit orb; like a lone jackal lamenting its dead cubs. I vented all the horror, grief, and madness that had welled up inside my half-crippled mind. Yet still I knew the moon silently gloated, and that it had guided me only with evil purpose. Then I almost believed I could hear its laughter.

* * *

I had lain for some while, gazing into nothingness with tear-filled eyes. As yet, I had taken no note of my surroundings, for there had been much turmoil within my mind upon completing my ascent of the steps. Now, as I remained motionless, there came to my ears the vague sound of melancholy voices carried on the eternal breeze. And the trance-like quality of the hypnotic music came with exquisitely crafted words and I thought that surely I could be listening only to the sad laments of angels for the threnodies were very solemn and most beautiful.

So I rose to my feet and found I stood amongst a wilderness of gardens; stunted trees with leafless, withered branches lapped at tiny pools of crimson with thirsting roots; hedgerows of black blossom defied the cruel moon's light, their pungent death-scent hanging in the air like invisible veils of sadness. Then, at odd whiles, caressed by the breeze, each blossom would sway and sigh like a host of grieving mourners. Then I realised I stood within Rahyani, the Perfumed Gardens of Death.

I walked upon a narrow stone pathway and crimson roses wept tiny blood-red tears at my passing, bowing to the earth as though at prayer. Dead nettles tangled with black orchids and seemed to be striving to blot out the light of the baleful moon and beneath them all reigned a darkness blacker than Shaizan's soul. And as I walked, I saw a female figure in repose beside a mist-shrouded pool of red, her slender back resting against a decaying tree, stunted and dying. Sad eyes gazed upon me a moment before losing interest, then her pale hands lifted to pluck the strings of the lyre she held. Her melancholy voice rose like a soul ascending to heaven to sing a mournful song:

All alone I sit in the twilight gloom
Voices of the damned call me to my doom.
All I do is cry a single tear.

Darkness in my dreams, shades of night must fall,
On misty wings it seems, I hear the night winds call.
All I do is cry a single tear.

I feel the soft embrace, of Eternal Night,
Soft against my skin, bathed in pale moonlight.
All I do is cry a single tear.

Hear my silent scream, lost in the deepest dark,
Blood upon my lips, poison in my heart.
All I do is cry a single tear.

The dirge faded as I walked further into the gardens, though the song tore at my very soul, its haunting beauty and heart-wrenching melody causing me to weep in sympathy for her doomed soul.

Presently I found myself beside a carmine stream; pallid white willows hung down from the banks like thirsty camels craving water. Then, even as I watched, their bland colour slowly turned to a vivid crimson. In other places black tomb-like monoliths rose up into the eternal night, but when, in curiosity, I neared one of these towers, a green luminous light suddenly flickered to life within a crystalline chamber atop it. Inside, a bloodless corpse peered down from the sharpened stake, upon which it was impaled, while gusts of mournful wind sighed like the souls of spirits in unrest. And from a grating in the wall of this tower came once again the haunting notes of a harp, filling all the air with sweet sadness. Then the pale lips of the corpse moved to sing its own weeping song, and the dark beauty of it all kissed my face with fresh tears.

In memory still there clings to me
My distant life that used to be.
A lingering love in my cold heart
No farewell kiss before we part.

These falling tears are all I know,
Decaying skin is all I show,
For life's now gone and all I see
Is your sweet face in memory.

I crave the sun, the warmth of life,
For in this place of dark and strife
My bones are cold, I ache to be
With you my love, eternally...

So when you dream, please dream of me
And hear this song I wrote for thee,
So you will know when you are sleeping,
I sing for you this song of weeping.

Again I passed on by, my ravaged soul screaming in torment. That these were tortures sent by Zhariman, I doubted not, but it took all my strength and willpower to resist their seductive lure. For I knew that if I stopped to listen to the songs of weeping, I would never find my beloved Zareena and free her from the malign grip of the Dark Way.

After a time the stone pathway crossed many others. Always I wandered onwards straying neither to the left or right, my mind caught up inside an intricate web of horror and beauty, bewitching my very soul with a whispering as of angels, but sometimes slyly spoken as with the voice of cunning Peris. Then I saw the mist had thickened, swirling strangely about the twisted trunks of dying trees, and in its haze I saw briefly a slender figure sobbing. And with this sight I again wept openly, experiencing all the stinging grief of bereavement for every heartbreak and loss I had ever suffered. For my eyes now beheld Rhazib, the Ghost of Sorrows herself, in her existence of eternal heartache.

Still I walked onward through hosts of death-black roses that swayed continually to the rhythms of a melancholy breeze. Here and there I saw rotting vegetation being helped in its decay by small rivulets of slime, and this slime seemed to possess its own sinister intelligence and the singular will to drain sustenance and energy from all forms of life. Occasional mounds stood proud of the blackened earth, and within these jellied forms I saw bones which had once held human life, now seized by the poisonous touch and burnt as though by potent acids -- absorption into a death that could never be true.

Down a slight gradient I walked, for I saw an area amongst the bare, stooping trees where the wind swept the roses into a black frenzy. Yet when I grew near this place, there fell a sudden calm, utter silence filling my ears with a void of nothingness as intense as a dying scream. I stood inside a small clearing, and here the bowed heads of the ebon blooms wept steadily, their crimson drops falling to stain the soil below. And falling quickly to my knees, I wiped wildly at the bloody earth with my hands until I gazed through the transparent surface of a tomb, and within it beheld a sight that nearly stole my reason. For within this crystal tomb reposed the pallid form of the one they called Sister Midnight, but in truth was my beloved Zareena!

Dead! Zareena was dead! I had failed. Utter anguish gripped me and for a moment despair threatened to devour my tortured mind. The universe around me seemed to totter on the brink of utter extinction and a void of unreason sucked at my soul. Zareena; vibrant, beautiful Zareena, dead and placed within a tomb, an innocent victim of this wretched realm!

And so it was that a strange mixture of rage and sadness gripped me. My rage was directed towards one creature: Zhariman! I would slay the Demon Lord even if it meant I should forfeit my eternal soul! I would rip out his black heart and lay waste to his atrocious realm. In anger, rage and sorrow I wept once more and it seemed the black roses wept also, but their weeping seemed to contain sly undertones of mocking laughter.

I then continued to work with my hands until I made progress enough to remove the crystal slab that sealed the tomb -- and in a cold rage I smashed its oblong form upon the ground! Then very gently I lifted the cold, lifeless form of Zareena from her place of undignified decay, carrying her carefully in my arms and vowing to myself that her body should be taken from this unholy place and be given sacred cremation within the Village of Heartbeats.

But as I began to carry her insensible form along the stone pathway, there came to me a sudden feeling of great foreboding, as though some malign force within the Perfumed Gardens of Death had now become aware of my stealing one of its own. I felt that hidden eyes secretly observed my actions from some place of concealment. So always I kept alert and intently observed all about me.

Now, after I had walked some little way along the pathways, my mind gripped in a turmoil of roiling emotion, I stopped and looked back towards the place of roses and strange mists. And for some minutes I remained thus in silent observation, mesmerised by those macabre flowers and their occasional swayings and leanings. Then I noticed a vague shape of blackness amongst the twisted trees. This, at first, I thought to be some strange shadow cast by the misshapen branches, for often the swirling mist was prone to cause distortions of moonlight. But very suddenly there came an unexpected thinning of the haze, which afforded me a much clearer view of what I actually gazed upon. And with this, I turned and walked rapidly on my way, for I knew that staring from the mist had been a figure that hungered for my body and soul: Ulasto Vidath, the Corpse-Keeper and Garnerer of Graves. His taut yellow skin appeared stretched and mummified, thus creating a visage that appeared centuries old, perhaps older than Time itself. His hollowed eye sockets gazed in my direction yet saw more than living eyes could ever see.

Once more I looked back as I carried the body of Zareena, this time seeing that the black-shrouded figure stood closer to me amongst the weeping roses. His cruel face looked toward the ransacked tomb where Zareena had previously reposed and he turned and immediately began to stride purposefully in my direction. At this, I began to walk swiftly upon the pathways, all the time searching for some manner of exit from this infernal place of mockery to all that is death.

In a little, I beheld the welcome sight of the garden's outer wall, but my relief was slight, for built within it I saw an ancient gate of bone. And the reason for my fear of this sight were the three fire-lit skulls which sat atop its archway, for their empty, glowing sockets of flame scorched deep into my memory, uncovering dreadful thoughts of Gorannon, and the malign spirits which haunted it always. So I looked for some alternative manner of egress, but saw only that the outer wall was of a very great height and too formidable to climb with my precious burden.

Again I saw the shrouded vision of Ulasto Vidath, walking very slowly but with determination in my direction, for now his unholy form appeared to stride in time to silent rhythms of death, as though the doom-laden music of funerals played always in his mind. And it was disconcerting to realise that, although the progress of the Corpse-Keeper seemed slow and ponderous, still the distance between us had grown no greater than before and I put this down to my sorrowful burden.

I made to increase my pace, walking very quickly toward the gate, yet as I made to pass beneath its macabre bone archway, I heard the flames briefly roar and then extinguish themselves within each skull-lit lantern atop it. Then high in the sky I saw the malign moon flicker and stain itself a deep crimson, while in that very second came a mournful howl from the far side of the estate. And the mists of the gardens appeared to be absorbed into the unhallowed ground itself and each stunted tree visibly bowed as though in reverence of great power.

Crimson moonlight fell to illuminate every part of the garden with its ruddy glow and now the absence of the mists afforded me a clear view of areas I had not before discerned. At the far end of the garden, stone steps led up to a darkened balcony that defied the blood-moon's glow; somehow it seemed fastened to a solid wall of Night itself. And leaning upon its rail was a dreadful figure caped in midnight-black, eyes blazing with the green fire of hatred, her presence harnessing all the darkest memories of long-forgotten Nightmare Tales. Pale lips drew back over small, pointed teeth, wicked and sharp, and once more she howled with a mixture of grieving and vile rage, her chilled voice reaching far out into the Everlasting Night, causing even the coldest corpse to shudder in its toil or unrest. I knew that I looked upon Mashyane, The Dark-Minded Mother of Death, standing upon the Balcony of Night and a thousand nightmares flapped and frolicked beneath the folds of her midnight cloak ever eager to fasten themselves hungrily upon the minds of humankind.

I turned my eyes from her venomous stare, and gripping the cold body of Zareena tightly, kicked and smashed my way through those brittle gates of bone which meant to hold me captive. Beyond the gate I met a well-beaten track that I knew for a surety led back toward Jilyah, the Village of Heartbeats, and in this direction I began to walk with a rapid pace.

* * *

Now, after some while spent in walking, there was a slow but steady dispelling of the crimson of the moon. And this was a great relief to me, for that orb of blood was most unsettling. But often I gazed back along the way as I went, always peering hard into the gloom and darkness of the track, forever seeking for any evidence that Ulasto Vidath followed in my wake. And though my eyes met with no sign of anything malign, still there dwelt within me a constant feeling of unease, for I knew not what malevolent spirit or sinister force may await me in this realm of Eternal Darkness.

Chapter X
Jeh the Beautiful

Strange the charm of her purple eyes,
    Like pale moons that shine;
O sweet the taste of her painted mouth,
    Sweeter than rare wine.
Her cheeks were soft as lotus blooms,
    A demon shapely faced,
And graceful were her wand-like arms
    And snake-like slender waist.
Her locks, which stung like scorpions,
    Along her cheeks, were bent:
The rondure of her hips and thighs
    That quivered as she went.
Her radiant face it dimmed the light
    Of the opal moon,
Her beauty lit the endless night
    Like candles cleave the gloom.
If man should steal a furtive glance
    And gaze into her eyes
Demon-bolts will sear his soul;
    He'll fall and never rise.

Zal in the Land of Demons

EVENTUALLY I APPROACHED Jilyah, and never would I have thought those strange, vaulted buildings and sinister houses to be such a welcome sight. But truly it was so and I was most relieved to be entering the Village, for the evil within The Perfumed Gardens of Death had been awful in its intensity, and I felt that I should never be free of its grip. Though when I walked amongst the streets of the Village, I found them to be once more deserted and this made me the more wary for any sign of the Dead Ones.

When I came near to passing the large domed building of 'entertainment', I heard the sound of much laughter and excited feminine shrieks from within, and this I took to be a sign that the vile 'show' I had been told of was now underway. At this, I found myself gripping the cold body of Zareena tightly, for I knew the dreadful Akomar now went about his cruel act, working under the name of Alazaar. And only when I had walked some good distance beyond this place did I feel more at ease, but I knew now the Dead Ones were undoubtedly in Jilyah, so I walked ever cautious and very guarded.

After a brief time, I found myself in close proximity to some of the smaller domed buildings, and though I was alert to the state of my own safety, still a great curiosity came over me once more. And it happened that when I walked past one of these strange buildings, I noticed that a crack of light emanated from inside; for a curved outer door had been left slightly open, thus affording me the perfect opportunity to view the mystery within. So, very cautiously I walked over to this place, putting my face up to the gap and peering inside. And what I beheld behind the door, of a surety only the cruellest and most callous mind could ever render. For affixed to the inner walls of the dome were tiny bone cradles -- and within each lay a newly born babe! Yet the real horror of the dome dwelt in what was taking place inside, for central to the cradles stood a crystalline figure of Zhariman, and from out of the open mouth of this blood-filled image emerged many small tubes of crystal, each one attached to the tiny wrists and necks of the helpless babes.

I came very near to crying out in horror at such an abominable sight, but from behind the unholy image of Zhariman came a sudden movement, and this caused me to quickly regain my sense and realise the dreadful danger I was in. For walking slowly around the inside of the dome I saw one of the black-shrouded Dead Ones! Occasionally it would lower its decaying face near to the sleeping form of a child, almost as though it revelled in the sound of its young heartbeat. At other times I saw the sickening bone fingers close about the loose flesh of a child's torso, seeming to measure the development of the body and the excess fat. And within these seconds there came the dreadful realisation of the purpose of these small domes, for their function could only be the breeding of the young, thus creating a constant supply of babes. Sickened I held the form of my beloved Zareena against me and moved onward, my tears falling to wet her frozen cheeks.

* * *

The awful sights within the small dome had heavily disturbed my mind, and I walked rapidly, despite the weight I carried, until I reached the area of the Village comprised solely of the sinister tomb-like houses. Yet all the time I walked, there remained within me the constant feeling of unease I had known for so long. And on occasion I would glance back upon the way I had come, almost expecting to look upon the visage of the Dead One I had witnessed inside the breeding dome.

In a little, I made to rest a while, so carefully I laid the cold body of Zareena beside one of the houses some distance from the main street. But as I lifted my head to gaze once more upon the way I had walked, I became filled with a terrible anguish and fear. For again I looked upon the venomous figure of Ulasto Vidath, his slow stride still taken in rhythm to the solemn funeral beat eternally filling his head. And now there was borne upon me a terrible realisation, for it was clear that if the evil of The Perfumed Gardens of Death could reach out this far beyond its barriers, then it seemed I had no hope of keeping the body of my beloved Zareena from its blasphemous unrest. I made to draw my sword but the cold gaze of Ulasto Vidath fell upon me and my hand slackened upon the hilt. Despite my intent to draw my scimitar and slay the foul creature that sought to desecrate the mortal remains of my beloved, I backed away, giving up her frail body to the malignant Corpse Keeper. The vile sorcery of Ulasto Vidath had usurped my will and although I realised that Zareena's corpse would never be cremated as Perushian custom dictated, I could do naught but observe in shame as the Corpse-Keeper approached her body.

Ulasto Vidath came to a halt and stood over the body of my beloved and his fleshless face turned in my direction for some seconds, almost as though he silently considered whether further pursuit would be required, but in one very quick movement he fell to his knees beside the corpse. Then I became both sickened and outraged, for the hollow-cheeked face of Ulasto Vidath neared Zareena's own pale visage and his cracked lips and jutting jaw opened to breathe the foul breath of corruption upon her own sweet skin. And though I was a distance away from that awful spectacle, held motionless by the uncanny will of the creature, still I saw the flesh of Zareena's face instantly decay. Swiftly I turned my face away from the wretched sight, for I did not want to witness the Undead Kiss. So I turned my eyes upwards toward the gloating moon, and vehemently did I curse my great stupidity, for once more I had overlooked Al Pharazeme's own doctrine that death could never truly be the end.

So, after the departure of Ulasto Vidath with the corrupted body of Zareena, I walked from Jilyah freed from the bonds which had bound me to my quest and my mind was numb with sorrow, for now I realised that pursuit of the Corpse Keeper was fruitless and that Zareena's soul could only be saved from the curse of the Dark Way by the death of Zhariman himself. Then my sadness became mixed with much anger.

* * *

After a time my aimless perambulations took me to an area of dire appearance. There grew about me black poplars and huge twisted yews; each tree standing in silence; like disapproving sentries. These dark trees of death grew gnarled and distorted, their contorted boughs echoing human limbs that threshed in the throes of extreme agony. It seemed to me that they stood in an avenue, which receded before me, and that their very movement was an enticement to walk down that contrived pathway. Now it came to me that the light within the avenue of sombre trees grew very dim, but still my sight was drawn therein and I perceived, standing at the far end, a place of dwelling. Still, I could not help but take note how the illumination of the building was singularly vague and indistinct, and though this created a certain amount of unease within me, still I could not help but feel attracted to it. Now, for some while I stood and considered retracing my path, but I was not disposed to return to Jilyah or The Perfumed Gardens of Death. Therefore I made the decision to travel between these foreboding trees of dark despair towards the evil dwelling place. So it was that I began to walk down the path flanked by the poisonous trees towards the mansion, and I ceased not walking until I reached its door.

* * *

The vast house stretched up mightily and was girthed with a balustrade of red veined black marble supported by statues of colossal demons and Jinn, their hideous faces fashioned into aspects of evil, their sharp, wicked fangs and hard eyes shining cruelly. There were many windows, some draped with purple cerements, others unadorned, but within each sinister void lurked darkness. Then I turned my eyes toward the portal which stood before me and I soon came to notice the door knocker, cut from a single piece of jade and carved into the aspect of the grinning face of a ghul which gripped a great brass ring within its evil jaws. So I grasped the ring and lifted it. Then I felt within me a mixture of trepidation and anticipation as I slammed the ring down onto the ebon wood of the door and a dolorous booming sound echoed within the mysterious building. For some seconds I waited until the door was slowly opened to reveal within, cloaked by shadows, the slender form of a veiled maiden. She moved forward into the uncertain light and I beheld a creature whose visage was more beautiful than the Houris of Heaven. Her ebony eyes, khol lined and sparkling, shone with the light of a billion stars and her full ruby lips, discernible through the diaphanous yellow silk of her veil, were as red as fresh blood upon mountain snow. Her forehead was flower white, her cheeks pallid as dead flesh; her breasts like pomegranates of even size, rose and fell like the waves upon the shore of a sunless sea and were as pale as lizard bellies. Her features were delicate as finest pearl and her raven tresses dark as a demon's heart.

I stood entranced, for such beauty ravished my soul. I forgot all I had endured of perils and sufferings and was seized by a lustful desire that overwhelmed all reason.

With a languid wave of a delicate hand she bade me enter the shadowed mansion saying:

"Greetings, Khalik, I am Jeh, I bid you enter my humble abode."

And thus it was that I entered the Mansion of Evil.

* * *

I stepped across the threshold and found myself in an immense hall. In many areas the ceiling and upper walls were obscured by dripping shadows, but at odd whiles these would part, affording glimpses of balconies and balustrades where curtains of chiffon trembled and swayed, as though parted by unseen hands. It came to me that these balconies were perchance inhabited by unseen watchers, perhaps Dead Ones or ghuls, gathered here to behold my fate.

Black candles in chandeliers and candelabras of fused and twisted bone cast a dim and dubious light that managed to conceal more than it illuminated. In dark corners indistinct shapes slouched and kneeled and I perceived sullen crimson eyes glaring at me with malevolence and hatred.

But none of this concerned my bemused and entranced mind for the enchanting beauty of the woman before me overshadowed all else.

As I gazed about the room movement caught my eye and I saw an oval mirror standing against a far wall. Its curiously carven frame was wrought from twisted gold and within the black glass I beheld my own image, thin and emaciated, with bloody, tattered apparel, but with a grim spark burning bright within my eyes. I surmised that Jeh no longer stood immediately behind me for her reflection did not appear within the shining glass.

Presently I felt a hand grip my elbow as Jeh grasped me gently but firmly and guided me into an adjoining chamber. As we entered, my nostrils were greeted with the savoury odours of all manner of meats, rich and tantalizing, and delicious and generous wines. I discerned a large table upon which had been laid a sumptuous repast, a banquet that would put the feasts of the Caliph himself to shame. All manner of dishes were displayed before me; spiced meats and rare pastries; exotic fruits and delicate sweetmeats and all manner of viands such as I had never looked upon in all my adventures and I did not even have knowledge of the names of most of the dishes, much less their nature.

Now Jeh gestured to a large chair at the head of the table and motioned for me to sit upon it. This I did, making to gaze upon the collation of provender before me, and at this time the fire of hunger made as to burn my very stomach, while thirst, too, set all my throat aflame. For too long had I dined on those loathsome blood berries, thriving on their unholy sustenance. And as I sat thus, Jeh seated herself upon a jewel-encrusted throne at the far end of the table, and with an enigmatic smile, gestured that I should eat.

* * *

Now as my teeth tore at the tender meats their warm juices dribbled down my chin, and so I ate as though I had been possessed by a slavering ghul. Then I thrust handfuls of succulent roast peacock into my mouth, ripped from its bed of dressed and peppered rice; these I followed with sausages and stuffed cucumbers and broiled lamb and grilled ribs of mutton and vermicelli with nuts and honey and fritters and almond cakes. Still ravenous, I continued by eating fried colocasia roots, soaked in honey with nuts and almonds and fruits and conserves and sherbets and jellies.

Time seemed to pass quickly, for my attentions were still focused solely upon my frenzied feeding. Then, in one startling instant, there came the sudden crashing sound of a gong, its reverberations passing throughout all the hall and, looking up from my repast, I saw Jeh wave a slender hand. Following this, the strains of exotic music began to emanate from some hidden alcove and I could only conjecture who or what the mysterious musicians might be. Then, from behind silken hangings, there emerged three females, concubines by their apparel, or lack of it. I saw that they were green skinned and brazen eyed: the costumes they wore consisted entirely of jewels and precious stones that twinkled and shone like the myriad stars of Perushia's skies. So it was, as I resumed my meal, that these three women began to move and sway hypnotically in time to the seductive melodies and counter rhythms of the music, and all this while their jewels and stones continued flashing in the seductive light of lamps and braziers. Their hips, moving ever sensuously, became as a magnet to my eyes, while constantly their arms were fluid and graceful as cobras. Small pointed tongues flicked, snake-like, between their full purple lips as they moved and gestured obscenely. The rondure of their hips and thighs intoxicated my soul, for their poisonous beauty was such as to put to shame the concubines of the Caliph. Desire within me was ignited but still I feasted upon the dishes of viands before me, for I knew not if I would ever again have occasion to enjoy such a repast in this realm of death and decay. But as I ate my gaze returned to Jeh who sat upon her throne, her small hands cupping her face. She did not partake of the food before us, but sat and watched me with a certain amused disdain.

Suddenly the primitive music ceased and the dancers glided silently back into the curtained alcoves. But by now my passion was greatly inflamed, for my lustful eyes gazed upon their shining emerald flesh as they departed, and I noted how seductively their thighs and buttocks moved. Of the food I had eaten a sufficiency but I now felt a new craving...

* * *

Jeh rose gracefully from the table and, gesturing for me to follow, disappeared behind a hanging carpet of rare and splendid workmanship which depicted a scene at once erotic and depraved. Urgently I washed my hands in the bowl of scented crystal water provided and, rising up from my chair eagerly followed her way. Drawing back the hanging carpet, I saw that she stood within her boudoir.

The room, I saw, was obscured by clouds of billowing smoke, which wafted and fumed from burning braziers placed about the walls. The pungent odour assailed my senses. But I could not tell whether it be the libations of rare wines I had imbibed or the powerful drugs and spices continually burning that now confounded my senses.

And it was then I began to fully appreciate what a vision of rare beauty Jeh was. For she stood there, illuminated by the caresses of the moon, which shone through a latticed window high up within the wall, and the flickering light of the braziers and lamps. Her eyes, deep and dark as a courtesan's secrets, turned towards me. Then she removed the veil from her face and for the first time I beheld her awesome beauty fully revealed.

Now it seemed to me that my heart had stilled within my breast as I gazed upon her. For the sight of her beauty choked the breath in my throat and the radiance of her eyes cast shadows upon my soul. Her lips, I noted, were swollen with her arousal and they parted slightly as her small tongue flicked between them for a second. As I stood transfixed, my blood racing and my body tortured by the searing flames of unbridled passion which raged within me, she smiled and raised her white hand to the golden clasp that held her robes. This she undid and the silk slid softly to the ground, caressing her body as it fell. As she did so the mists billowed and rolled and cloaked her, seeming to reveal and accentuate her nakedness rather than conceal it. Her breasts, I saw, were globes of ivory, from whose brightness the moon borrows light; her thighs smooth and round and white as pearl. She was the loveliest creature I had ever beheld and put to shame the fairest Houris of Heaven.

So it was that a burning fire of passion now raged within me and my reason was ravished. For a second the visage of my beloved Zareena appeared in my mind but it was in an instant transformed into the beguiling loveliness that was Jeh.

Being intoxicated by her incomparable beauty and well warmed with drink I moved towards her, casting my clothes and scimitar about me as I walked and not another thought did I give to my Zareena, though I had braved all the perils of the Night Eternal in my love for her.

Now it was, as I lay naked with Jeh upon the carpets of her bed, that I pressed against her and at once I smelled the delicious fragrances of musk and jasmine. Then, as I brushed my lips against the soft, warm flesh of her neck and our bodies joined in passion, I could not think otherwise than that I was in Paradise!

* * *

Awareness returned to me slowly, for my mind remained thick and heavy with the effects of imbibing too much wine and inhaling the intoxicating fumes within the bedchamber of Jeh. For a while I lay still, my throat parched and my head pounding, as I brought to mind the events of my night of lovemaking, and in that time all the horrors of the Night Eternal were forgotten as I bathed in the warm memories of our evening of lovemaking. And truly I felt myself to be in an oasis of pleasure in a never-ending desert of pain and damnation, or perchance lost in the mazes of an opium dream. So it was now a joy to be able to lie and bask in my good fortune; especially after all the horrors and tortures I had endured thus far. For I was in no wise eager to return to my quest, and Zareena, who seemed but a vague memory to me now, was undoubtedly lost to the Dark Way. Rather I would dwell here awhile with the beautiful damsel Jeh, spending my days talking and feasting and my nights locked in the embrace of love.

Now I felt the weight of Jeh lying on the carpets behind me and turning, I put out my hand to caress her warm tender flesh, for my memories of the past evening had aroused my passion, and once more my lust was inflamed.

A thrill of horror ran through me as my questing fingers encountered coarse, wet flesh, this being abhorrent to the touch and cold and clammy as the tomb. Then, overtaken by more anxiety, I turned quickly and saw with horror what lay by my side.

In an instant I jumped to my feet and searched for my scimitar, which I remembered, I had hurriedly cast aside in the amorous abandon of the previous evening. Of it there was no sign, so I looked down at the sleeping creature that still wore the lovely visage of Jeh, and lay entwined within the carpets and silks of the bed. At this sight my gorge rose within me from excess of loathing, for I realised I had conjoined with this abomination in the act of lovemaking.

Her corpulent body, I saw, was fully exposed, and the great expanse of her flesh fell in fold upon fold of rolling, quivering fat. Her huge breasts, purple veined and bruised, lay upon her fleshy stomach like overripe melons, and the teats of these leaked a sticky black fluid that gave off a charnel reek. Her semblance was that of a pallid fat maggot, bloated and over-fed on cemetery flesh.

It was as I stood and stared at this monstrosity with loathing, an obscenity made even viler by the beautiful face that it still wore, Jeh slowly opened her eyes and gazed upon me. But now I no longer saw the shining jewels I had gazed into the previous evening. Instead I saw burning orbs of blood red with pupils of white; they radiated a tangible evil that chilled my very soul.

Now did Jeh's fleshy, taloned fingers reach out for me, and with her delicate tongue she moistened her lips and smiled wickedly. Then it was with a lascivious gesture and a glint of amusement in her crimson eyes, that she parted her huge thighs and gestured obscenely, inviting me to enjoy her once more.

Disgust and repulsion consumed me as I gazed at this horror, for I could scarce entertain the idea that I had lain with such a creature and known her kisses and warm embrace. So I grabbed my shirt, breeches and sandals and fled naked, clothes in hand, away from that chamber of abomination. But as I ran into the dining chamber my repulsion doubled as I beheld the table, for this still held the remains of my sumptuous repast of the evening before. And truly I tottered on the black abyss of madness as my mind reeled at the sight before me. For there, on plates of yellowed bone lay, not meats and pastries and exotic wines but chunks of rotting cadavers, unmistakably human in form, bowls of Jazur Berries, and chalices of fetid, gelid gore. I saw teeth marks in the decaying flesh that were undoubtedly my own and saw that much of the dead flesh had been partially consumed. And as I stood there, transfixed by the absolute horror of my revelation, I chanced to catch my reflection in the dark mirror. With this I noticed my nakedness and rapidly drew on my clothes. Again I gazed again into the mirror, which held some strange fascination for me, and of a surety I should have fled that loathsome mansion. For I saw my reflection shimmer and ripple, as if reflected in dark, fathomless waters. Then the ripples subsided and I beheld my image replaced with that of Zhariman, the Demon, laughing with insane glee at my plight.

And so I screamed in anguish and turned my face away from that warped visage, then I fled from that Mansion of Evil, realising as I ran that I had left my scimitar, my only weapon, behind me.

Chapter XI
The Valley of Silence

There are many shadows in the Valley of Silence; black spectres of doom, dripping from the wings of night. By no sun are they cast, no, nor moon, but motion they have as they ebb and flow and endlessly dance to the subtle, torturous threnodies of the empty silence.

The Shah Nurmal, Book V

SHAKEN AND DISGUSTED to the very core of my being by the occurrences in the Mansion of Evil, I walked with no real awareness of direction, yet always was I bitterly ashamed that the memory of my beloved Zareena had been banished so swiftly from my thoughts. And though I knew I had been under the terrible enchantment of Jeh the Wicked, still this knowledge did naught to assuage my agonising guilt. Wrapped in my despondency, I know not how long it was I walked, but after a time I came upon an area flat and barren of features. Beneath my feet the ground had once more taken on a sand-like texture and, by the light of the treacherous moon, I saw nothing but a blackened plain stretching out far before me. There was no sign of fire-pits or fissures, just a silent and ominous area of great foreboding, and so I knew I had come to Shendi, the Desert of Desolation.

So I walked onwards through the perpetual silence, and such was the emptiness and constant cold of this place, that I entertained many thoughts of intense strangeness, for at times my body seemed like a thing that moved from habit alone, with no conscious effort on my part. And very occasionally the moon would flit behind black clouds, and when it did so I walked onwards in total darkness. Then truly, at these times I would think of myself as no more than a disembodied spirit doomed to eternal wandering on these plains of blackest night, and this state of mind enabled me to ponder most profoundly upon my plight. Thus I recalled the visions I had experienced in the Pavilion of Sunrise, and I thought of how the sun had attempted to rise and light the black skies above the Night Eternal, only to die a death so violent that it shook all this demonic realm.

After deliberating for some while, I began to feel a deep sorrow for all the unborn days that had died so suddenly and painfully, for I realised the multitude of scorching flames I had witnessed bursting outwards in that final explosion were perchance akin to their own dying souls. And mayhap the soul of Daylight itself had flickered and died in the Eternal Night.

* * *

For what seemed like several parasangs I walked through the dark and cold, and once more I felt the pangs of hunger and fatigue, yet I would not dare rest until I had found a place of true safety. And this seemed to be almost impossible, for even the vile moon had now grown tired of teasing me with its hateful beams, for the skies above were ebon black, so that I stumbled like a pitiful blind man, arms stretched out before me, senses ever alert and harking for sounds of danger in the vast night.

Now, eventually there came to me an awareness that I was no longer alone in the dark, even though there was not the slightest sound transmitted to my ears, and always my eyes saw naught but the utter blackness. Yet despite these facts, I could not help but feel that something now *listened* in the silence, as though some sinister entity lurked in the Night and constantly watched my progress.

After a little more time spent in walking, the sinister moon began to once again emerge from its cloak of clouds, and with this came the notion that I was now to be tormented by cruel glimpses of the horror that lay in wait. I thought of my scimitar abandoned in the Mansion of Evil and cursed myself for my stupidity and unfaithfulness to the memory of Zareena. Then by the dull light of the moon I saw that, just a few paces before me, the ground sloped down to an immense valley.

The panorama I now looked upon appeared spectral and forbidding, for upon both ridges of the valley were mighty boulders which threw the blackest of shadows despite the moon's dullness. But now my mind and body were very weary, so that the only option I had was to enter the valley, for the thought of returning to the desolate sands of Shendi filled me with a great horror.

Once more I cast my eyes over the dusky landscape, taking in the sight of the huge boulders upon the ridges and those surrounding areas of utter blackness. With this

I experienced a sense of unseen danger, and whether this stemmed from my new awareness of the workings of the Night Eternal or was a deceit of Zhariman's, I did not know. But I did know that the only chance of passing safely beyond the valley would be to descend, taking a direct route upon its floor and ascending the far side. So, very carefully I began my way downward. But beneath my feet were pieces of black shale, which slid treacherously with almost every step I took; and the harsh sound of the shifting rock caused me much anxiety, for it seemed as though the breaking of the constant silence would alert the unknown denizens of the valley to my presence.

Now, as I completed the final part of my descent, it came to my notice that the air was growing steadily warmer, and this was a great relief to me.

Soon I began to walk upon the floor of the valley, which appeared dusty and dead save for a small rocky outcrop toward the centre that I determined to make towards. But all the time I walked, it seemed the deathly silence that surrounded me held some sinister presence; and I felt that this presence had now become aware of my spirit, seeking to stifle it by way of the evil manifest all about. So it was that a sudden thought caused me a feeling of intense dread, for truly it could only be that this dire place I walked through was none other than the Vale of Mazrur, which some have known as the Valley of Silence.

Yet now I had no choice but to walk onwards, for my fatigue was such that I knew I had no hope of scaling the opposite valley wall without rest. So I walked slowly on towards the outcrop of rock I had chosen, hoping to locate some place I may take my rest in relative safety.

But as I made my slow progress, I suddenly felt a great depression overwhelm me while despair tainted my heart, for it seemed like a million years of silence pressed down upon me as I walked. Yet always I tried to resist these emotions, for, of a surety, I knew them to be no more than an *external* influence, and that it was the malign force within the valley that sought to corrupt and destroy my very spirit.

Very soon there came an indication that whatever evil dwelt within this place was growing in its power, for as I strode upon the dead floor of the valley, I began to fancy that I felt occasional movement and vibration beneath my feet, and this caused me great concern. For in my mind grew nightmare visions of the whole valley opening up beneath me and plunging me downward into the black heart of the Night Eternal itself.

Presently, I became amazed to hear a deep murmur of sound shatter the silence of the valley, which seemed to me like the heavy roll of distant thunder, but its noise was prolonged and held a continual note of threat -- never did it lessen in volume and fade away, but remained constant, seeming to be a low growl that always filled the vale.

When eventually I reached the location of the outcrop, I at once found a place amongst the boulders to afford me shelter from the eyes of the Dead Ones, or any other malign forms that roamed in the dark. And here I laid my fatigued body down. Yet from a gap between two boulders, I was able to look outward at the valley ridge to my right, for this was the place I would make my ascent. My tired eyes looked upon the places of blackest shadow being thrown by those immense boulders upon the ridge, and I discerned what I took to be clouds of steam rising upwards into the pale yellow moonlight. And all the while came that deep growl of thunderous sound, but I cared not what may await me on the ridge and my body slowly gave way to sleep. My last thought was to wonder if a sleeper could ever wake again within the unholy Valley of Silence, a valley that was silent no more.

* * *

But it was very abruptly that I did wake, for a loud thunderous sound shook the entire valley, which was then repeated three more times. It seemed to my newly wakened mind as though the whole Night was alive with angry Jinn, but though I stood swiftly and looked all about me, I could see no sign of danger or movement. But in the aftermath of these unexplained sounds the dreadful silence returned, and now it seemed to intensify once more. Then to me came again the uncanny thought that some dark presence listened always for even the slightest sound.

How long my time of slumber had lasted I did not know, but though my body now seemed in a more refreshed state, still I needed some nourishment. So once more I swallowed my shame, and I began to search the shadowed areas beneath the boulders of the outcrop for the Jazur Berries. And in finding that which I sought, I have to confess that I became less sickened than before. Though still I forced myself into silent prayers for those poor souls providing my sustenance... and then the Jazur berries did stain my tongue with their crimson juice.

Now, when I had eaten a sufficient amount to stave off the nagging ache of hunger, I at once made to continue in my travelling, for I felt that the malign force dwelling within this valley now seemed to have become aware of my presence. So I walked as far as I could within the cover of the outcrop, then I passed once more into the open plain of the valley floor. But in only a few paces there came again that low, insistent growl of sound.

And as I walked onwards with this terrible sound filling my ears, there began to grow in me a surety that its origin was in that hidden region high up on the valley side to my right. And so I turned my head and looked full upon that place which had always caused me such feelings of terror, determined that I should gaze full upon whatever horror dwelt there with my own eyes. But as I studied that area of deepest blackness, I beheld two lambent green flames spring up from the ground, and it seemed to me that the malignant eyes of the valley itself were studying me.

Without further pause I continued in my progress, focusing my attention upon the way before me in the uncertain light, but now I felt my mind had been contaminated to a much greater degree, for constantly I pictured images of a large blackened face with emerald eyes of burning hatred, and it was a surety that the continual roar of sound I heard could only be the angry growl emanating from its unseen mouth. Then, in one instant I realised that this macabre vision of mine was in truth no vision at all, but most surely was the creature known as Maruk Lith, the Watcher of the Valley, as is written in the *Shah Nurmal*. And truly, it is a fact that I could not help but turn my head that way once more, and there *did* appear to be some kind of a vague outline in the darkness that matched a face. In the following seconds I became pale with fear, for I knew that this vision was not a thing of my mind's creation but a very real denizen of this vile land.

Now in the following seconds came a great roar of awful sound, which violently shook the ground beneath my feet, and echoed throughout the entire valley. Concurrently there came the opening of myriad fissures of green flame in that place of darkness upon the valley side, as though a mouth of fire were forming beneath those glaring eyes. Then, even as I watched, I saw many glowing segments falling outwards and down the valley side, as though its fangs were loosened by the incredible power of that demonic voice.

Then once more the Voice of the Valley reverted to the continual low growl I had become familiar with, but now I knew beyond doubt that Maruk Lith had awakened and was aware of my presence within His vale. With this I began, at once, to walk in the direction of the opposing valley side, meaning to travel very swiftly and place a great distance between this new threat and myself. Several times I turned to look back upon those segments of glowing fire expelled from the mouth of the Watcher, for now each one had fallen downward to the valley floor, their emerald flames shimmering weirdly in the dark.

So I walked rapidly wondering if the Watcher was a servant of Zhariman or if the creature existed independently, springing from the venomous heart of the Night Eternal itself.

Now, it was amidst such ponderings of mine, that I once more glanced back at the Watcher, and with this I became very curious, for the shimmerings of green flame had reached the valley floor and still seemed to be in motion. I remained rooted to the spot for some seconds, peering keenly at the shimmering green fires until I came to the dreadful realisation that I looked upon the emerald flame-lit outlines of many corpses, each one moving across the valley floor in my direction; and with this awful fact came the understanding that Maruk Lith had now sent forth a small army of the dead, and that it was me they sought!

* * *

I then walked for an inestimable period of time, often looking back upon my way, observing with trepidation the unceasing stride of the Valley's Own Dead following my trail in relentless pursuit. For I realised that each cadaverous form was animated by the baleful will of the Watcher, and that every flame-lit corpse sought my destruction. But I had now reached the opposing valley side, so, very quickly did I began to ascend. Though after only a short while I realised that my slow ascent would lead to my certain capture, for the Valley's Own Dead never slackened in their speed. Yet still I made my way upward for a good while. And when I reached a small area of thin ledges and loose rocks, I looked back once more, becoming desperate with anxiety when I saw the figures of the dead were beginning their own ascent just beneath me.

In great despair I began to scramble over the smaller rocks, for even if my capture was a surety, still I would put all available energies into a spirited resistance. And in the following seconds there came a dim sight which brought to me a semblance of hope, for within that ledge I had reached, there existed a darkly shadowed area possessing in its floor a barely discernible opening. But still I approached this with caution, for I had already gained much knowledge of the sinister ways present in this realm, and maybe this was but one more trap. Yet once more I glanced downward, and very quickly I determined I had no option but to enter this opening, for the Watcher's Own Dead were close at my heels.

Now, the cavity I stood before appeared barely wide enough for the body of a man to pass through, and this reassured me greatly, for it would be most difficult for the Watcher's Own Dead to follow me. And so I carefully lowered myself into the darkness it held, hearing a muffling of the awful growling as I passed within. So it was that I began my way downward, but the total blackness I moved in came as a great disadvantage, for always there was the necessity to find my way by the use of touch alone, and many times I grew greatly concerned lest there be a sheer drop awaiting any mistake in the footing I made.

Very soon I came to realise that my descent was, in actual fact, a marginal one. This being so, it was very likely that I made my way into the valley side, rather than straight downward. But my progress was slight and I could still discern the faint glow of the venomous moon through the entrance. And though I hated that pallid orb with all my heart, still it brought a vague reassurance to me, for at least I knew of the valley its pale beams fell on. So it was that I continued to struggle inwards for some good distance, until I began to feel some measure of safety. With this, I made a decision to rest a while, for I had found a protruding slab of rock with size enough to accommodate my body.

Then as I remained in my state of repose, I heard the distant fading and eventual termination of the ominous growling. Once more the following silence seemed filled by a quality of great tension, as though some sinister happening was very soon to occur. But my concern at this moment was of the Watcher's Own Dead growing near to the entrance of the opening, so I prayed that the darkness of the shadows would conceal the entrance from their corpse-eyes. But as I gazed upwards at the dim glow of the moonlight in the entrance, it was suddenly filled with the grim vision of a flame-lit countenance; green orbs of fire peering from the sockets of a skull, slowly searching every inch of the interior darkness for my presence. Then suddenly those dreadful eyes fixed on me, staring downwards from that body beyond death; so that I could have screamed with utter terror when I saw its face of charred flesh and crumbling bone smile with ghastly delight!

Chapter XII
The Sirens of the Night

Our voices enthral, come, list to our chant.
Our songs are as sweet as the honeycomb flowing.
Our melodies twisting like the tails of serpents.
Our sensuous mouths sing songs of dark rapture.

The Siren Song – The Shah Nurmal, Book VI

IN THE VERY second those corpse-eyes lo-cated me in the darkness my mind became gripped with such terror that my only thought was to hurriedly escape the evil gaze. And so I quickly scrambled from the slab of rock, but in my haste I lost my footing and slipped. I fell but a short distance through the darkness before my body slammed into a solid flat surface.

Yet still in my mind lingered the vision of the flame-lit skull-face which had peered down at me, and suddenly a strange thought occurred to me, for as I now recalled those orbs of green fire which had burnt in the hollow sockets of the eyes, I could not help but make comparison with the demonic eyes of Maruk Lith. For it seemed to me they were but lesser versions, as though the Watcher now gazed outwards through the eyes of the living dead. I knew then that the green flame surrounding the corpses in some manner caused their locomotion and that Maruk Lith dictated their actions.

And so I realised that these bodies of death were nothing more than extensions of the Watcher itself, creatures made of death and evil walking abroad from its very mouth to do its bidding. Then my spine shivered in fear as I thought of how the corpse-face in the entrance of the hole had smiled evilly downwards, for it was as though I had witnessed the Watcher's own face smile with satisfaction at my predicament.

In a little, I climbed to my feet, but reaching out my arms in all directions, I found I could no longer feel the close confines of jutting rocks. Even the vile moon had deserted me, so that I stood in an area of utter blackness, with no way of knowing if, even now, the corpse that had spied me was making its own rapid descent. So, very carefully I began to move deeper into the darkness, but as I took my shuffling footsteps, my sandals began to kick against loose chippings of rock upon the floor. With this action there came many terrible moans echoing all about me, as though countless souls of the dead cried out in the dark.

For some seconds, the dreadful sounds of plaintive sighings and tortured groans continued to fill my ears, making me feel as though I had now unwittingly entered a vast underground chamber which could only be inhabited by the unquiet dead. But eventually these sounds grew fainter and then ceased, so that once more I stood alone in the constant silence and utter dark. But the knowledge that this awful place was not uninhabited was of great concern to me, for, with no means of illumination, I would have no awareness of any danger that might await me within the ebon gloom.

Now, for some while I remained motionless for I felt no urgency or great need to make further progress, for my great fear was that the undead corpses of the valley had now entered into this place and would very soon locate my whereabouts. Then it was that as I remained in this state of silent pondering, I noticed uneasily that a flickering white flame suddenly illuminated a small area of darkness.

I crouched low and silently observed. It appeared to me, after a time of study, that the flame had sprung from the floor of the cavern itself. A pale patch of light fell over the area surrounding it, and yet I still could see no sign of movement or anything untoward that occupied that place. Thus I decided to very carefully approach, for still there was no knowing what dark secrets the darkness beyond may hold, and from those dreadful sounds I had already heard, I knew that it could only be something of warped and unholy origin.

But as I grew nearer the source of the light, I noticed with dread that it was no kind of flame at all, but rather the pale radiance given out by the petals of the White Lotus of Decay. A thrill of fear ran down my spine, but I was also gripped with much determination and anger, for I knew this macabre flower was the only one of its type, and that it belonged to Zhariman. Then I grew very wary lest I had walked headlong into a cunning trap, for I could not fathom why this illumination should be available to me at precisely the moment I had wished for it, unless it be that even now Zhariman lurked nearby, watching me from some place of darkest shadow. For how could the White Lotus of Decay suddenly come to be there, unless it had been placed?

However, I reasoned that it would be foolish if I did not seize this one opportunity to escape the darkness of this place, for how else would I ever hope to be able to navigate my way within the gloom and confront the myriad dangers it held? Perhaps this was to be the opportunity I needed to destroy the vile heart of Zhariman, thus freeing Perushia from the grip of the growing shadow? So, very carefully I bent over and lifted the White Lotus of Decay from the floor, my hand closing around the slim vase of bone that contained it. In the following seconds my curiosity caused me to examine the flower more closely. And so, peering through the pale glow, I saw each petal to be as white as corpse flesh, but gazing down the thin stem into the vase, I was appalled to see that it drank not from wholesome water -- but from gelid blood.

For some seconds I became greatly repulsed by my discovery, for truly it was a great blasphemy that such a thing had been created to nourish itself with the blood of the dead. Yet still I realised that I should overcome such loathing, and quickly begin my progress further into the cavern. So, very carefully I began to walk within the radiance of the flower, for those groans and whimperings I had previously heard within this place, had already informed me that it could only be occupied by some variety of suffering form. Though perhaps it was that those pitiable sounds were devious entrapments, for this is ever the way with the inhabitants of the Night Eternal.

For some while I walked onward through the cavern, navigating many windings of the way and several rockfalls. But always keeping my eyes keen for any sign of threatening evil, for I suspected that Zhariman remained very near to me, and that he had chosen this place to bring about a confrontation to cause my destruction. Then it was that, as I made progress around one curvature of the way, the floor before me gave into a steep gradient downwards, and a great chill was in the air.

So I walked slowly down the slope, and the radiance from the White Lotus of Decay began to illuminate the darkness. But it was in the following seconds that a vague whispering reached my ears, becoming gradually more audible the further I walked. And for some while I remained motionless, listening intently to the whispered words that travelled through the darkness. Then came a pause for some seconds, though very suddenly the whispering began again. And the words I listened to were spoken in the form of a poetic prayer, but the voice held a quality of cautiousness, as though knowing some terrible punishment would result from being overheard.

O Gods above please have a care
For in this prayer I hardly dare
To speak aloud, for it is true
My soul is trapped and screams for you.

So hushed I speak "please stop the cold
And all the darkness I behold"
I'll softly plead though it's sin
From this grey stone I'm trapped within.

A million dreams of life I knew
Of love I had that was so true
They're fading fast to black and grey

Into this Night that hath no day.

Zallah above, I know not where
I speak to you within this lair
Of dark and cold, and hope you'll care
To listen to my stolen prayer...

I felt a great sorrow at hearing the words of the prayer, but still I remained wary and alert for any sign of evil, for the notion came to me that the prayer had been skilfully contrived to evoke a deep sense of sadness in anyone that may hear it. So always as I walked I peered intently into the area of radiance cast by the White Lotus of Decay.

Soon, the gradient had levelled out, and now I came to sense very strongly that some awful *thing* lay very close by, concealed within the darkness. With this, a mounting level of fear grew within me, so that every fibre of my being told me to turn quickly and retrace my steps. But to do this would mean certain capture by the Valley's Own Dead. And it was in the following seconds that I heard a sudden sigh, as though of deep sorrow. So very quickly I looked about, and saw only that the radiance from the White Lotus of Decay illuminated naught save the encasing rock, yet as my gaze briefly passed over the cavern wall to my right, I shuddered with great shock. For frozen into the very stone, I saw the body of an old man.

Just to behold such a sight was a cause of great distress to me, for it appeared his body had *grown* upwards from the floor and merged with the living rock of the wall. I knew this man, who should have lain at peace in death, was now tortured beyond it. Then I saw by the light of the flower, that the flesh of the man had taken on a grey sheen, akin to the colour of the stone itself. His arms had somehow moulded themselves in such a way that his hands were raised in the manner of prayer, and protruded from the wall.

I was most ashamed that I had ever suspected this poor soul of a contrived evil, for suddenly I saw his grey eyelids open and staring out from the wall were solemn eyes, attempting to focus in the glowing radiance of the flower. In a moment a look of great rapture filled the face, but very shortly this was replaced by one of grave concern, and very softly came the enquiring whisper from those thinnest lips of grey:

"Saviour or Shaizan...?"

And my sorrow was so profound that I could not reply, for how could I, a living being, ever hope to understand such a suffering as I now beheld? It was clear to me that the man's eyes had now become blinded to such an extent that they could only barely see the radiance of the flower. As I walked slowly away, I saw they closed once more. And trickling from beneath the grey lids came tears of scarlet sorrow.

* * *

I had walked some good distance further when my ears became filled with many deep groans, sounding as though they carried not just the agonies of eternal suffering, but also a great quality of bitterness and threat. They were so menacing as to create within me uneasy thoughts of a whole army of savage corpses, each existing just beyond the radiance of the flower, waiting impatiently to rip any warm-blooded human to shreds.

I walked onward into the darkness for I saw no gain in remaining motionless or retracing my steps, for both these courses of action would undoubtedly bring about my swift capture. So I moved on, ever alert for peril, and it was only a little way further when I looked upon the horrendous sight of many corpses that had grown upward from the floor and moulded into the very walls of the cavern. And as I walked nearer these tormented souls, their partially sighted eyes would become aware of the radiance from The White Lotus of Decay, causing their moans to grow much louder, and various distorted words to be uttered by those that still remembered speech. These words I heard were not just pleas for aid, but also very threatening; as though the dead tried to intimidate me into coming closer to them. And I did not dare dwell on the purpose behind this, for this vile place had often taught me that the dead could hunger beyond death.

It was very soon that a new threat began to grow apparent to me, for I saw that occasional grey arms had broken free of the walls, and yet still these held the power of movement. Then, as I continued in my progress, there came a gradual narrowing of the cavern, until eventually I fully realised my danger, for occasionally arms would swing outwards in the direction of the flower. And many times would I begin to feel the touch of stone-cold flesh, as their hands would lash out and try to grasp hold of me, while others tipped with sharp nails would claw savagely in my direction, often slashing painfully through my skin. I staggered on through this nightmare of grasping hands, my lacerated body close to the limit of mental and physical endurance, sobbing heavily and sending prayers to Zallah that I would not be slain by these sorrowful creatures of darkness.

And as I staggered onwards, thinking my life had reached its end, it seemed my silent prayer had been answered, for very suddenly I felt a slight breeze upon my face. Then the groans of dire threat and pleading came to an end, so that I realised I had passed beyond their limits, and now had come very close to stepping back outside into the Night Eternal.

Now, it was in only a little while more that I came to see the beams of the hateful moon falling through a gap that would afford me exit. And this stirred a mixture of emotions within me, for I was loath to admit to myself that any pleasure could be gained from the sight of that ghastly orb. Yet in its beams I lay my battered body, thinking to rest a short while before I journeyed again beneath those blackened skies of death. As I rested I wondered about the whereabouts of Zhariman, and why the White Lotus of Decay should have been left for me, as though meant to afford my safe passage. But it was in this time of contemplation that my eyes grew very heavy and the shades of sleep crept over me.

* * *

Very suddenly I awoke, and it almost seemed that a voice had spoken to me only seconds before my waking. Still I remained in the same position upon the stone floor, but upon looking outside the cavern, I was amazed to see the moon no longer hung in the sky, and everything without had now been shrouded with deepest darkness. And so, for some minutes, I remained upon the floor within the glow from the White Lotus of Decay, and I was very glad of its comforting light.

The utter silence outside the cavern became broken at times by the sighing of little breezes, and these seemed to hold a quality of intense isolation and cold beauty. Then, on one occasion, it happened that a wandering gust of wind entered into the cavern, playing through my hair like a soft caress, and causing even the strange light of the flower to dance as though in great delight. And as time went on, I heard the sighing of other little winds, whispering with a strangeness which could almost be interpreted as many voices, very beautifully calling through the dark. Eventually I became certain that, on occasion, there would be feminine voices of remote beauty; yet no actual words were distinguishable to my ears, but only the sweetest whisper to entice and soothe with haunting tones and gentle melody.

I remained entranced by the voices; it seemed as though the Night itself called out to me, bewitching me with a quality of beauty and love that was equal to all the evil and suffering I had so far experienced. And though I knew of the trickery and all the malign ways employed by the Forces of Evil within the Death Realm, still I listened to the soothing whisperings, for there surely could be nothing malevolent about such a form of exquisite sound. With this, I took hold of the slender bone vase containing the White Lotus of Decay, and I made to walk outside a little way beyond the entrance of the cavern.

Once outside the cavern, I found that I stood upon a sloping hillside, though beyond the radiance of the flower I could see nothing but pitch-blackness. Yet still I heard the bewitching sound of many sweet voices carried on the wind, and so I made to walk warily in the direction from which they emanated. In a short while, I noticed that the ground began to level out, and it was only a little way on from here that I halted in my progress, attempting to gain more idea of the area from whence the voices came. But in the following seconds I cursed myself for the stupidity of a child, for in an instant every bewitching voice had faded to silence, and simultaneously the radiance from the White Lotus of Decay expired. Then there came to my ears a sound dreadful beyond all I had known so far -- for it was the voice of the Night itself, and it was the sound of cruel laughter!

Chapter XIII
The Galleries of Sublime Suffering

Mayhap they are pieces of the Night: black shards ripped from the ebon belly of the sky. Their crimson eyes smouldering with hatred they lope across the twisted landscape of the Night Eternal, for they are the Jat-Su: the Hounds of Darkness

The Shah Nurmal, Book IIX

THERE NOW DWELT within me a strange mixture of fear and anger, for though I cursed myself for having fallen prey to the malign influence of the Night while I had slept, I still remained greatly concerned at the consequences of the trap I had fallen into. Upon noticing I still had the White Lotus of Decay held in my hand, I quickly threw it to the floor and made to smash its vase, meaning to take some satisfaction from destroying such a prized possession of Zhariman. But with this act of defiance, it seemed the whole Night became enraged, for it was as though all the Forces of Evil abroad in the Night Eternal *seethed* with silent anger.

I crouched within the darkness while the intense silence pounded at my ears. Yet in the following seconds, I heard something moving towards me. At this, I looked over my shoulder -- and shuddered at the awful sight I saw! For the flame-lit outline of a shrouded corpse drove a pair of savage, demonic horses pulling a macabre carriage fashioned of blackened bone. Marking its outline were rows of bleached demon skulls, hollow eye sockets flickering with deep-red flame, like luminous blood.

So I covered my eyes to prevent the horrific sight, yet still I heard the sound of the carriage draw to a halt beside me. Suddenly came the sound of the coachman stepping down from his seat, and the ominous creaking as he opened the carriage door. Then I felt the cold touch of the scorching fire that surrounded those long-dead hands as they lifted me bodily within. Seconds later I heard the crack of the whip upon the horses then the wind sighed like souls in unrest as the Black Carriage carried me away.

We passed through regions where fire-columns struck upwards from the charred ground where indefinable forms crawled around their base like demented demons worshipping at altars of scorching flame. In the glow of many fires I saw occasional grotesque buildings; like sinister cathedrals designed by insane minds, they stood like beacons of some forgotten inimical religion. At times I heard haunting snatches of orisons but I dared not ponder upon what dark proceedings took place behind those opaque windows. And soon there came the voices of rotting corpses; the charnel stench of ancient graveyards; the presence of soulless phantoms, and the gathering mists of deceit.

Once, when I looked out of the carriage, I beheld large black shapes that loped alongside; the red fire of hatred within their eyes, and the splintered bones they held within their slavering jaws, leaving me in no doubt that I looked upon the Jat-Su, the terrible Hounds of Darkness. And I knew, of a surety, that these terrible beasts sought to devour my soul. At that time it seemed to me that their very bodies were of blackness that could only be made up of the Night Eternal itself. But it was as the first loping beast drew alongside the carriage; the largest of the pack, that I perceived they were indeed hounds of flesh and blood, though whether they truly lived I could not say. Their hides were dark as the abyss and their coarse hair was matted with filth and offal. And now the snarling pack had surrounded the carriage. The largest beast then made a mighty lunge at the carriage door, its wicked claws snagging on the protruding bones of which the door was fashioned and pulling it open as it fell back. Then swiftly into the carriage came that savage beast, the fetid breath from its open maw filling my nostrils while its crimson eyes flashed with wild triumph. And truly it seemed to me that my doom was at hand for I had no weapon. Yet in that moment when it seemed my death was inevitable, there came to life in me an outrage at the hound's intrusion, and into my arms flowed a strength that seemed inhuman. And with an automated movement of swiftness unparalleled, I seized the front legs of the hound and wrenched them apart with a mighty force that burst its foul heart. Even as that dire form slumped lifeless did I lift its body within my hands and cast it from the carriage, then angrily slamming shut the door. And at this the baying of the remaining Jat-Su immediately ceased, turning instead to hungry snarls as they gave up the pursuit of my carriage in order to fight over the body of one of their own.

* * *

Eventually the carriage began to slow. With this, I looked outward to see the sudden return of the blasphemous moon, its hateful beams falling through the darkness to highlight the ruins of a cemetery and the dark outline of a most sinister church. The carriage jerked to a halt, and seconds later the door at my side opened, though the coachman still remained seated, and I stepped down from the awful carriage. But now my fear of all the unknown horror within the Night Eternal again prevailed, so that I ran toward the tangle of shattered tombstones hoping to find some place of concealment amongst the wrecked graves and areas of darkness. But as I ran I chanced to look back towards the carriage, and from atop it, the blanched skull of the coachman turned my way, and from the darkened orbs within his fleshless countenance projected a silent form of evil to snatch away my consciousness.

* * *

The pungent odour of death filled my nostrils as consciousness returned, and raising my head, I found I was lying where I had fallen, amidst the desecrated graves in the cemetery. I looked over to the church and saw the sign of the Evil One burning brightly on the outer doors in the dark. I felt intense fear then, for I knew this to be the Church of Shaizan. From within, I heard the cold, hateful voice of the Prophet, screeching to those encased in a death that could never be true death. Hatefully he blasphemed the Creator, Mazura Ahara and Heaven, and the stupidity of mankind. Then he said: "Go forth and gather!"

The outer doors creaked slowly open, and emerging from within, I saw a procession of six black-shrouded Dead Ones walking solemnly in pairs. Ahead of them strode Jalur the demon, his small, twisted frame waddling self importantly as he twirled a yellowed femur with the greatest dexterity. Upon his bloodless face showed a smug smile of pleasure at being afforded such an important role. Along steaming pathways they made their way towards me. Once I tried to stand and run, but an abnormal ache had now frozen my muscles to immobility.

The wan face of the moon gazed down, observing all with distorted delight, and glinting in its pale light, I saw those cowled visages of ancient bone moving through the dark. They came to a halt just before me, circling and lifting me with hands of bone, onto their shrouded shoulders. Forming once more into three groups of two, they carried me into the deeper areas of darkness, until we reached a place where steps of bone led down into a veil of blackness. Following Jalur, we began to descend.

There was no light as we walked and it seemed those cold hands of Death now fully controlled my destiny. I felt helpless, and it seemed as though my entire quest had unfolded to some dark design unknown to me.

Eventually our descent came to an end and I was carried into the glow of fire-torches, my breath frosting visibly in the sudden presence of underground cold. To my ears came the sounds of many sighs and groans and to my nostrils the presence of a death-stench with a putrid quality greater than I had known previously.

Suddenly a terrible feeling of dread filled me, for we came to an area where an awful, candle-lit figure sat behind a desk of blackened bone. Then the Dead Ones let me to my feet, but still I hardly dared to look upon this figure, for I had no doubt that this time I looked upon the genuine visage of Akomar, the Torturer, and this was no mere magical projection which filled my sight. A cape of blackness fell over stooped shoulders, while blood-red eyes gazed outward from a lurid face of sallow corpse-flesh; He peered through the darkness as though in detailed study of my very mind and soul.

A pale hand lifted upward from the surface of the desk, then a black-taloned index finger motioned me forward, as though a sinister, parent now summoned forth a troublesome child. In the next instant the cruel tones of the Torturer spoke.

"You have dared to defy the Night Eternal and the unholy will of the Dark Way; you have sought to destroy Zhariman, and all that he represents. Thus you have now been summoned, and it is my decision that you shall be made to look upon the Galleries of Sublime Suffering, and shall be made to know of the Deformed Creatures of Coldest Cruelty. Then shall you be absorbed into the very heart and spirit of the Dark Way!"

With his last shouted words, Akomar brought his white fist crashing down hard upon the surface of the desk. Again I was lifted upward by the cold hands of the Dead Ones and Jalur once more led us into areas of utter darkness. Soon we passed through a barely perceivable door, and then began to descend another stairway, this having those same death-black walls, lit only very rarely by the occasional fire-torch. But as we descended, there once more came to my ears many hideous screams of agony and these grew in volume the deeper we went.

Suddenly we came to an abrupt halt in an area that seemed to have levelled out, then those hands of long-dead bone flung me forward into the dark -- and at once I felt my body slam into a door that opened inward. Once beyond, I quickly turned and sought to do battle with my captors, but now all I touched was a wall of blackness, which seared my skin in the manner of the fiercest flame. As I nursed my hands in the darkness my ears filled with the most horrendous of moans, so that I hardly dared to turn and take in my surroundings. Yet when I did, I looked upon a sight of dreadful cruelty, for all the walls about the room were made up from the deep blackness of the Night Eternal, and nailed to them, burning with a never-ending pain I saw a multitude of ravaged corpses, each one alive-in-death.

Now, as I walked through the Galleries of Sublime Suffering, I beheld many terrible scenes of anguish, causing me much emotional distress. I felt intense sorrow and pity at all the grim sights and sounds I experienced, for occasionally impaled sufferers would call out to me for succour I could not give, and this upset me greatly. But truly, it is a fact that this macabre place was much like the dungeons beneath Al Pharazeme's own palace so that I then wondered if these black manifestations were in some strange way linked to the Caliph's catacombs of horror.

The similarities between the two dungeons also carried as far as the extraction of blood from bodies. So once more I looked upon the sight of small crystalline tubes carrying blood, but this now seemed more like an indifferent gesture, for such was the small amount of Heartbeats, that surely this could never serve any great purpose at all?

One thing that puzzled me greatly was the continual existence of icy draughts that filled this dark place, for I knew these dungeons were built far beneath the ground. And this was just one of many things I could not explain with any surety, save perhaps the chill emitted by the walls now reached outwards, and sought to encompass other things, a characteristic common in many substances and themes throughout the Death Realm. But it was while my head was filled with these ponderings, that suddenly I noticed the awful groans and sounds of suffering were becoming quieter, so that when I again looked upon the walls of blackness, I saw those many tortured bodies were now some way off in the distance.

As I walked onwards, I noticed the only light afforded me came from the very occasional fire-torches. In their glow I saw the crystalline pipes that carried along the extracted blood of Heartbeats, and I knew a great curiosity as to its destination. With this, I decided that I should follow the course they took through all the dimness, for perhaps this would be the only way of escape from this dread place. I trailed these macabre pipes until somewhere ahead of me I made out a larger area lit by four fire-torches. And the sight these afforded me came as a very great shock, for once more I looked upon Zirik Mobol, the Crimson River.

As I grew nearer Zirik Mobol I saw that the river emerged from an area of deepest black. Yet steadily my vision became clearer until I was able to see a small shallop moored to a bone securing-ring. A little way beyond this area, I saw the crystalline pipes were now trickling a slow flow of crimson to the greater mass of the river. At this the thought came that the constant flow held some defined usage, yet what this could be I could not conjecture. And while I puzzled over this matter, there occurred something to cause me instant surprise and alarm, for very suddenly there came a brief flicker of white radiance, giving light to a distant area of the river previously shrouded in black. And then I had no idea if what I gazed upon was real or another sorcerous trick by a sinister denizen of the Night Eternal, for it seemed to me the light had revealed the baleful view of Zhariman; his form stood upright inside another floating shallop, which somehow defied the river's flow and within his outstretched hand he held the White Lotus of Decay!

For some while I considered the vision I had observed, and whether this had been a thing of reality or perchance another magical conjuring, since there was always trickery and deceit within this realm. It was obvious to me that my weakened state would prove less resistant to these sly ways. Though still it dawned on me I should investigate the area the radiance had illuminated, and if the meeting between Zhariman and myself were to take place there, then so be it, I was ready!

So I took hold of the rope attached to the shallop, and pulling it toward me, stepped from the wharf and onto the rocking boat. Then I slipped the knot from its mooring, thus giving the small vessel up to the will of the river. And as the shallop began to move downstream, I made examination of its interior, looking for its small oars. Instead I found it to contain nothing but two empty crystalline containers and a small bone bowl, this holding a handful of Jazur Berries. And so, being ravaged with intense hunger, I began to devour the Berries very greedily, though it is to my shame I offered no prayer to Zallah for the souls of past humanity affording me this nourishment.

Now, very soon the river carried me from the glow of fire-torches and into areas of deepest dark, but the effect this had was most passing strange, for my mind began to grow clearer now, as though much of the inner horror became soothed by the blackness. But this I suspected to be another sinister trick of the Night Eternal itself, so that I tried to remain very alert to danger. And for some while I kept my eyes keen, intently watching the dark for the slightest glimmer of light, but deep within myself I suspected that Zhariman had not appeared in the physical sense at all, but had thought only to tease and lure me by way of a magical conjuring.

* * *

After some time spent travelling through the dark, I became aware that there existed some imminent danger, though how such an awareness came to me I cannot say, unless perchance my mind was becoming attuned with this vile Night Eternal. I peered through the surrounding darkness thoroughly, and yet I had not the slightest idea what it was I sought. But soon there came to my attention a weird glowing of orange flame having the shape of an orb and in dimension being the size of a human head. This glowing orb approached very slowly, at times hovering just above the surface of the river, its orange radiance reflecting horridly from the crimson surface. Then, faster than my gaze could follow, it transferred to another position, all the while maintaining a constant backward movement to preserve its distance from the shallop. And all this caused me the utmost concern and puzzlement.

In the following seconds I saw the fire-orb closing the distance between itself and the shallop. And with this I was soon able to discern a darkness within the orange flame, which appeared to be the visage of a charred face, constantly observing me from within. The orb came to a halt at a length perhaps two paces away and I saw eyes of utter blackness staring fixedly at me; the orange glow now stretching out to surround my own head, and its touch felt akin to a sensual caressing hand of fire! Yet before I could even cry out in pain and disgust, the orb had retreated into the darkness. Then everything was calm and quiet once more, and it was almost as if the bizarre incident had never occurred.

Now, for quite some length of time I pondered upon this strange event, but it came to me that there was still much about the malevolent powers of Zhariman and the Night Eternal that remained a mystery to me. It seemed to me, however, that the orb was some macabre, sorcerous means to recognise Heartbeats and corpses that travelled the river, by identifying their visage.

For some inestimable period of time I was carried by the flow of the river, my mind ever wondering what my destination would be, and very suddenly I became amazed to see more fire-orbs moving through the darkness ahead of me. With this, I suddenly became very curious, and so always kept my gaze upon the movement of the orange orbs. And it so happened, that when one passed nearby, I was allowed a closer examination and, for one brief instant, my eyes looked upon the sight of another charred face, but the mouth of this one was wide open in a silent scream of torment. At that, I became cautioned, for I remembered that all things linked to this dread place are subject to laws of subtle cruelty, as this was often used as a method of control. Thus I knew these orbs to be the Ruz Shamral, the Faces of Torture.

The question immediately entered my mind as to why the Ruz Shamral paid me no heed, and the only conjecture I could make was that each was joined in thought and deed by the magical power of Zhariman and that all they perceived was in an instant known to the Demon Lord. But quite disconcerting was the realisation that I had been allowed to travel onward, for it could only be that my way corresponded to the wishes of Zhariman, the current of the river conforming to the will of the Night itself, as though my way forward were a granted evil blessing.

Now, it was only some short while later, when I beheld the sight of bright fire-torches and the flickering of eerie green lamplight. With this, I kept up a constant observation, soon becoming astounded to discern many shallops moored to a wharf, and further back the lighted windows of sinister tomblike buildings. So it was that I suddenly became very apprehensive, for now I remembered Khostrau's mention of this dread place, and I knew the current to be carrying me into the port of Pharezeum.

CHAPTER XIV
THE FROZEN REALM

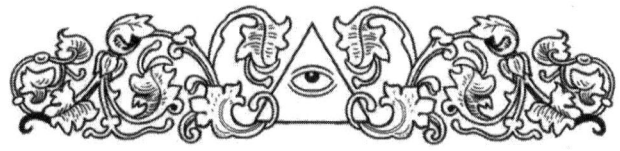

Banks of steaming clouds billowed out towards him, and from the depths of the glacial scarps came a blast of freezing wind that sought to pluck the very air from his lungs. And then he beheld Alhamdul, an immense pyramid of ice and he knew that within this awesome structure there dwelt a creature of supreme evil, for Alhamdul was the Pyramid of Vile Intelligence.

Zal in the Land of Demons

AS I GREW nearer to Pharezeum, I saw the sight of many figures outlined in the glow of fire-torches; these moved slowly and clumsily in an awkward rhythm that lacked the easy gait of living men. With this, it was clear to me that the whole port was, of a surety, populated by those of the Undead, each one plying their macabre trade in utter silence. Soon I made out the stiff movement of corpses unloading shallops, or pulling small carts along the wharf.

So it was that I thought my capture to be a surety, for, as I have already said, my strength had now deteriorated so much that I would be able to give only limited resistance. And as I approached nearer to Pharezeum, there came from it an icy chill that seemed to pervade my very soul, reminding me somewhat of the unaccountable breezes and currents within the Galleries of Death. Then very soon I came in proximity to other shallops secured along the wharf, fastened in rows like floating tombs awaiting occupants.

Within occasional shallops would burn the light of green lamps; the glow affording me a gruesome view, so that I saw crystalline containers of blood; bone bowls containing Jazur Berries and black baskets of culled flesh. Others contained weakened figures of death, many slumped over and seeming too enervated to leave their boats. I wondered then if the dead sleep.

I passed this area and my shallop grew nearer to the wharf itself. Now I remained with my body hunched over so as to not be instantly recognisable by the toiling dead as a figure of life, though always I kept my eyes slyly turned towards the wharf, for there was much morbid curiosity in me concerning this terrible port. It was but moments later when my small craft came to a halt by scraping against the side of the wharf. And it was then that I thought my capture to be a surety, so that I turned my head in expectance of the dead approaching, ready to fight or run, but I was surprised and greatly relieved to see no attention was paid to me.

Minutes passed, and I noticed those of the dead that did look in my direction would soon look away, as though nothing out of the ordinary was to be observed. At this, there came to me the gradual realisation that my appearance must now be so emaciated as to look most corpse-like. And although this insight caused me to shudder with revulsion, still I saw how such a fact could be used to my advantage. So, very slowly did I begin to move, as though hampered by atrophied muscles, though in truth my muscles were indeed withered and my former freedom of easy movement was now a thing of the past. So, carefully, with the uncertain and lethargic gait of the dead, I climbed onto the stone steps by which my boat had come to rest, and ascended to the wharf.

Taking slow, hesitant strides, I walked out among the crowds of the dead in Pharezeum. And this whole experience now became bizarre in the extreme, for those gaunt occupants about me toiled in a variety of tasks, seemingly against their will. For very often I would see weeping figures sat in doorways, shaping bone or weaving human hair, while others unloaded shallops or pulled small carts along the gloomy streets leading away from the river.

Then, in a short while, I came upon a narrow alley between two vast buildings of dark stone. These edifices were tall as the minarets of Sharador and held many crystalline windows lit by green lamplight. Gazing through one such window, I saw that within there were vast store rooms containing many strange and macabre objects, so that I looked upon all manner of stuff, such as brocades and embroidered cerements fashioned from human skin; mound upon mound of plump Jazur Berries; accoutrements and furnishings of blackened bone and twisted sinew, large jars and chests of rotting corpse meat; crystal decanters of gelid blood and an abundance of sundry items both macabre and ghastly.

Moving on I found myself walking down a dimly lit street, and in an alcove ahead I discerned a small congregation of the Undead illumined by lurid crimson lamplight; then, growing closer I became sickened when I beheld the emaciated corpses of naked women. They moved lasciviously and lustfully in ways they thought would seduce and entice, their flaccid breasts and hollow hips swaying as they danced -- but this lewd activity brought only shame to them, and pity and remorse from me, for I remembered well my meeting with Jeh the Whore.

And then I became aware of the presence of the Dead Ones.

In the darkest of shadows they stood, their black death-shrouds blending perfectly with the thick gloom; their yellowed bone faces barely discernible, but constantly watching. Suddenly, through the darkness behind me there came a snarl of sheer hatred. In terror, I turned in the direction of the sound, my hand instinctively going to my waist for my lost sword, and I saw the form of a pale, naked corpse staggering towards me. Its lips were drawn back over rotting teeth and its grasping skeletal hands stretched out in my direction. And in those dull corpse-eyes was the undoubted knowledge that I was still a man of life.

My salvation came from a most unlikely source, for moving with the silence and rapidity of phantoms, came the sudden intervention of the Dead Ones. Two of the dark creatures silently descended upon the screaming corpse, their black-taloned hands stretched out to rend and tear. Thereafter I can give no word as to what took place, for quickly did I retrace my steps back down the alley, though behind me I heard the ghastly echoes of ripping flesh and the abominable sounds of frenzied feeding.

Now, as I walked along, I wondered why the Dead Ones had intervened to prevent the attack on me, for never would I have thought to owe my life to such as they. I deemed it an act most worthy of suspicion for there was much wickedness and cruelty within this cursed realm and I could only surmise that it was the dark will of Zhariman that guided the actions of the Dead Ones.

Very soon I was walking along the main causeway of the port, mingling with the dead once more, but this time keeping my countenance toward the floor to give the dead no further chance of recognising a sign that life still dwelt within me. After some short time, I began ascending a wide stone staircase and this appeared to be a most popular route, for it was taken by many of the dead denizens of Pharezeum.

* * *

It was as I neared the top of the stairway that a great danger suddenly became apparent to me, for I noticed that my breath was frosting visibly in the sudden chill of the air. Now, it was a surety that if those walking beside me noticed this, then most certainly would my body be ripped limb from limb. Indeed it was a blessing that each dead form seemed more taken with their own melancholy state, and this introspection meant they paid little heed to that which was about them.

Then, as we reached the top of the slope, I saw the reason for the sudden chill in the air, for stretched out before me, vanishing into the gloom of Night Eternal, there lay a vast plain of frigid ice, and this I knew to be Kuruk Kulla, The Frozen Realm. I noticed then that the

Undead were falling into orderly lines, almost as though in accordance with some previously arranged instruction or unheard command and were shuffling out into the frozen wasteland. And it was at this time that I bethought me to make a break away from the main grouping, taking my chance that none would pay attention to one preferring to walk alone, for I noticed that there were several of the Undead doing just this. But to my dismay I saw a number of them form a line behind me and begin to follow in my footsteps. Still, I thought the plan to be a sound one and left the host with as much speed as I could achieve whilst still maintaining the pretence that I was of the Undead.

I managed to make some distance from the main host of the Undead before pausing to look back. The corpses that had sought to follow me had also left the horde and were now standing in a state of confusion, for I had outdistanced them most rapidly. Then I became aware of two of the Ruz Shamral moving rapidly towards them out of the distant gloom, skimming rapidly above the surface of the ice.

It seemed the Ruz Shamral had somehow become aware of the errant corpses leaving their comrades in death, for they at once descended upon them and I watched in horror as they hovered above the liches and enveloped them with their orange aura. As the glow washed over them, the Undead fell to their knees writhing in pain and screaming in utter torment.

For some while I remained motionless in the gloom, thinking it was a surety that the Ruz Shamral would inflict the same form of discipline upon myself, but it was not to be so. Instead, I saw the evil glow of those Faces of Torture leave each supine corpse, and as the victims rose shakily to their feet the hovering skulls grouped them together and herded them back toward the main throng as a shepherd herds his goats.

The fact that the Ruz Shamral had overlooked me came as a great relief, but was also of much concern, for it seemed once again that my destiny was in the hands of the Demon Lord.

The ice field before me was featureless. In every direction save behind me the wasteland was unbroken until the gloom hid all from sight. I had no desire to return to the Port of Death, so it was that I had no alternative but to walk on across the frozen fields with the host of the dead. I reasoned that by keeping their walking forms within my range of sight, I would be certain to discover their destination, but would also have the safety of distance if it should happen that this place be another of Zhariman's foul traps.

Now, as I walked across the frozen realm, I would oft peer across to the organised lines of corpses that trailed their own way, always keeping my direction parallel with theirs. Alongside the lines of walking dead, I could see the glow from the Ruz Shamral, which had now grown in number and were allowing the dead no deviation from the desired route. And though I remained some way distant, I noticed that many of the corpses still pulled sleds, while others carried heavy burdens; these no doubt laden with similar macabre goods as those I had glimpsed in Pharezeum.

The harsh climate now began to affect me somewhat, for it had begun to snow and the wind was ever in my face with its cold caress. My progress became slower and my movements more sluggish, and now it seemed that the frigid air was freezing my very soul.

Occasionally moonlight fell from the cloudy skies to illumine this bleak and sombre place, lighting the surface of the ice with its cold light, while the sorrowful, moaning wind would continually sweep the snow in gusts and flurries. Yet still there was something in the solitude and dreariness which reached out to touch my spirit in a strange fashion, for it was as though a deep part of me felt at one with the sense of alienation.

So I walked onward for some good distance, and eventually the wind died away in one low, solemn howl. Then came a sudden brightness to the light of the moon, followed by the ceasing of snowfall from the black skies and an unnatural calm lay over all. It seemed to me this but presaged some new act of evil. And truly, as I made my slow progress across the frozen realm, the wind began once more and I saw that it blew the fresh snow from beneath my feet to reveal the ice below. I noticed then that the ice was no longer opaque but clear as crystal and, as the bright beams of the moon fell down to penetrate it, I saw to my horror that there were countless undead corpses frozen within. I thought then of the crystalline corridor running through Vouruskasha, The Sea of Sadness, and it was a surety to me that the eyes of each Undead one peered up through the ice, their frozen brains filled with a dark jealously for the warmth of the living.

And so it was, that I quickly made to continue on my way, for the ill will of the frozen dead seemed to taint my mind causing me great turmoil and hurt. Silently then I cursed those hateful forms that stared upwards at me through this invisible barrier of death.

I had walked some good distance before the ice became vacant of its frozen forms of death, and some short way after this, its surface again became opaque and white as corpse-flesh.

Once again I shuffled through the frozen realm, the throng of the Undead always within my sight.

After some time walking with my head bent low I chanced to look up, and at this instant the hateful moon broke through the clouds for its uncaring light to show me a sight so astounding as to stun the imagination -- for I gazed upon a vast pyramid of ice!

The progress of the corpses, I saw, was straight towards this bizarre construction. And though I had told myself I would approach no place within the Frozen Plain lest there be a total assurance of safety, such was the intrigue inspired in me by the sight, that I could not help but bend my steps in its direction.

* * *

As I grew nearer I saw that the pyramid was of immense proportions and that eerie green lights shone from within its translucent walls. These, I noted, seemed to be moving slowly inside the structure about a man's height from the ground.

Growing ever nearer I saw that the ice of the outer face of the pyramid appeared to hold a vast human skull that dominated the wall. I could only conjecture what terrible Jinni or redoubtable demon this skull once belonged to, and only marvel at the potent sorcery needed to convey it to and encase it within the frigid ice of the vast pyramid.

Also within the wall that faced me, situated directly within the gaping maw of the massive death's head, I saw there was a vast gateway. And I observed the main host of the procession of the dead being guided towards this opening by the Ruz Shamral, though I noticed that there were others of the dead being taken directly beyond it. I also noted that those of the dead taken inside did not pull sleds or carry burdens of any kind, and this caused me to surmise that some other structure, located beyond the mighty pyramid, must await those of the dead who carried or pulled burdens.

Now, as I came nearer to the pyramid, I saw that what I had at first taken for an immense skull was in fact a macabre network of human skulls and sundry ossuary remains, and it was these charnel artefacts that formed the chilling death's head. Now I saw another face of the pyramid and noticed that that too bore a tremendous skull within its face. Then I knew that all four faces of the pyramid were decorated thus, giving the uncanny impression that four gigantic faces of bone stared out unceasingly over the Frozen Realm.

Then I turned my eyes to the interior of the pyramid – for it was a fact that every area free of bone held the clarity of unblemished crystal - and saw that upon the floor countless rows of the Undead lay motionless, as though frigid with cold or fear. Walking amongst these supine forms I also beheld the figures of ebon shrouded Dead Ones, sometimes lowering their silver lamps of eerie, green light to furnish illumination for greater examination of particular corpses. This explained the presence of the strange lights I had witnessed from a distance.

I was taken with a great curiosity as to the purpose of this pyramid, for unlike many other places within this realm of Night Eternal, there appeared to be no obvious means of torture or wanton cruelty; just the Dead Ones constant examination of those lain upon the floor. And I could only conjecture that perchance some preordained use was to be made of the corpses, but what this might be I could not surmise.

Looking upwards towards the apex of the formidable structure, I could just discern a huge interior mass of flesh-like blackness that seemed to continually ripple and reshape itself in complex, twisted convolutions, almost as though it possessed a strange will of its own. And I somehow knew that this was, of a surety, an enormous brain of vile intelligence, which plotted evilly, and which held a dark control over all within the Frozen Realm, even over the loathsome Dead Ones themselves. Then I shuddered at this thought, and made to continue on my way at once, for there was a great sense of evil emanating from that strange structure which seemed to permeate my mind in a manner most loathsome.

And thus it was that, very quickly, I made to continue in the direction taken by the Undead that did not enter the pyramid, but I found they were no longer within sight. So it was, that I walked away from the pyramid for some good length of time, only looking back when my mind no longer felt the disgusting caress of the vile brain. Then it came to me that the direful structure was no less than Ahlamdul, described in the *Shah Nurmal* as The Pyramid of Vile Intelligence. No other name could ever describe it so aptly.

I had left the pyramid far behind and was now alone on the frigid plain when the moon suddenly dimmed somewhat, leaving me cursing with anger, for now all about me was naught but frozen gloom. And truly, I must say that the venomous outrage and frustration I knew then was of a ferocity that startled me and I wondered if my mind had been horribly tainted by the touch of the vile brain within the pyramid. So it was that I had no option but to struggle on through the gloom, but now with no means to guide my progress.

* * *

I knew that I was hopelessly lost within the Frozen Realm, but continued walking through the freezing gloom, for I knew not what else to do.

After a good while spent in walking, I heard the sound of many little streams flowing about me. Then, stooping nearer the ice, I saw it was laced with myriad fissures all filled with crimson, as though a ghastly web of red veins covered the whitened surface. Then I knew a deep dread, for the dull light of the treacherous moon faded completely, and I became enveloped completely by the sinister velvet blackness of the Night Eternal!

I wanted to scream at the unforgiving darkness, but knew that was, of a surety, an act of madness, for I had no certain knowledge what may walk abroad in the night. So I stumbled onwards, though my progress was, of necessity, very slow and my mind was gripped with a great terror. I knew the cunning and slyness of the traitorous moon and I was filled with great dread and apprehension as to what the coming seconds would bring.

Then very suddenly a tremendous howl of sound rent the darkness, while at the same instant the traitorous moon once more broke through the ebon clouds. The sight I beheld then filled me with anguish and horror, for ahead of me I beheld Ahlamdul, The Pyramid of Vile intelligence. I fell to my knees in dismay at the realisation that, in the utter darkness, I had made my way back to that from which I had sought to escape. Gazing toward that hated edifice I noticed that the many skulls within the wall facing me now glowed with eerie life, for inside each dark eye socket there now smouldered a sullen carmine light. Then, as I watched in horror, twin beams of blood-red light sprang forth from each skull to pierce the gloom of the Night Eternal, so it was as if they searched all the darkness with their sanguine gaze, while all this time the terrible wail of sound emanating from the pyramid's interior continued.

The gaze of the pyramid travelled rapidly over the gloomy ice fields of the Frozen Realm and I did not doubt that I was the object of this search. As this thought came to me I saw that sanguine gaze approaching me: it would be only moments before the crimson light of Ahlamdul fell upon me!

I closed my eyes and offered a blessing to Zallah, for I felt it a surety that my doom was upon me.

When such was not the case, I opened my eyes and was shocked to see that, some way to my left another figure had been located by the questing gaze. And though this figure was some way distant to me, I saw it fall to the floor enveloped in the crimson light. Then I watched appalled as it writhed in obvious agony, before bursting into a glaring fireball of scarlet flame, which burned briefly, utterly destroying its victim.

Then the myriad twin beams began to move again and the eldritch gaze of Ahlamdul bathed me in its unwholesome light!

I knelt and awaited my doom, all thoughts of flight abandoned, for I knew I could not outrun that terrible gaze, and indeed I did not have the will to do so. But, to my puzzlement and great relief, the gaze of the pyramid left me and retreated swiftly back into the many eye sockets of the skull image from which it had originated. And it came to me then that perchance I had not been the object of the vile search.

Soon my eyes adjusted to the dull light of the moon, and with this came a sight that chilled me to the bone, for before me, only yards away, I saw a great chasm in the ice. The blood-red fissures and streams I had observed earlier had grown in size and all spilled down over the edge of the chasm creating a crimson waterfall, which tumbled down to colour the ice far below, gathering into small pools and trickling along in other newborn flows.

Then I looked back towards Ahlamdul, wondering if the eyes of the skulls had cast forth their crimson gaze with the express purpose of saving me; and I looked up to the moon, puzzled as to why it should reveal to me such a danger. But, as I have said before, the ways of the Night Eternal are beyond the small understanding of any man's mind, for always they work to further the cause of Zhariman and the Dark Way.

So I looked about me in study of the cliff of ice I stood upon, and I beheld a flight of steps descending into the chasm, fashioned from the solid ice of the Frozen Realm. These blocks of ice had been skilfully manipulated to form the strange stairway; a rail of bone held secure by frozen supports gave the only help to those risking descent. Yet this was, of a surety, the way I must go, for my only other option was to retrace my steps, and this I had no great desire to do.

So I walked to the place of the steps and very carefully began my descent, all the time gripping the bone rail very tightly and being most careful of my footing on the uncertain ice. But as I came to reach halfway down the stairway I saw with horror that, frozen into every remaining tread was the head of a Heartbeat. The ice had served to preserve their skin perfectly, thus capturing the final scream upon each pale countenance, and I knew those pleading eyes still gazed upwards with living sight... Then my own mind began to chill at the thought of the contrived cruelty put into this vile act, for anyone descending these steps was forced to concentrate on the security of their footing, thereby assuring that there could be no avoidance of the distressing sight. Yet I could not help but admire the sinister source of intelligence and cruelty that had rendered such a dark and subtle scheme.

When I eventually reached the bottom of the steps, after a most arduous descent, I made my way slowly between the pools and streams formed from the crimson waterfall and walked out into the gloom of the ice field.

I paused to look upward at the cliff behind me. In some areas I saw other crimson cascades of blood, some of which had now been frozen in many macabre visages of pain and torment, and it was as though a hundred bloodstained faces peered down at me in silent fury for walking upon the frozen skulls of their brothers in my descent of the steps.

* * *

For some good while did I continue my journeying across the Frozen Plain, leaving the bloodstained cliff far behind me. Then it began to snow with a great fury, and the wind grew also, so that I found myself bent almost double as I walked with much discomfort into the lashing storm. And many times did I think my blood had transformed to ice, such was the inner coldness of my body, but always I maintained my progress, ever thinking that a place of refuge might be just ahead. And truly, it seemed to me the very Night itself must have been secretly listening to all my thoughts, for suddenly the blizzard ceased and just ahead I made out a structure -- though it was not a surety that this would indeed be a place of refuge.

Before me was a pavilion of ice. Its size appeared much smaller than that of the vile pyramid Alhamdul, but still it was of a size greater than most Perushian palaces. Once more I saw the walls to be strangely translucent, so that I became filled with much trepidation upon my approach, for I wondered what new horror I would discover within. But still I could put no chains upon my curiosity, and heedless to any danger, I neared the icy walls. And indeed my apprehension proved to be justified, as the sight within the pavilion was such as could be taken from the blackest nightmare, for I saw many rows of decaying corpses strapped into seats of bone, each one struggling for release.

Each chair faced in the same direction, as though every corpse awaited the start of some dreadful show. So I turned my head to witness the unholy sight that caused their distress, and, standing before them upon the cold floor, I saw a large image of Shaizan, the Evil One shaped from blackened bone. The expression upon the charnel face was one of greatest hatred, as though the sinful image actually held awareness, its dark orbs staring malevolently at the corpses seated before it.

Once more it seemed I had walked to the rhythm of a terrible destiny, for at the very moment that I gazed upon that horrible image a strange event began to unfold. At first I thought that what I beheld was just some strange distortion caused by gazing through the substantial wall of ice, but moving to a nearer position, I knew for a surety that it wasn't... for the blackened mouth of charred bone was slowly opening and exhaled from it, into the frosty interior of the pavilion came the dark breath of the charnel effigy of Shaizan, rising into the air like effulgent sable smoke.

The dark breath coiled and twisted in the air, and I saw that the swirling substance was transforming, and that myriad horrific images were forming within it. To my eyes came the sight of demonic cathedrals; fissures of bubbling blood; weeping corpses; bodies moulded into stone; black roses, crimson moons of blood, carriages of bone, columns of fire, Dead Ones feasting, the Jat-Su baying, cemeteries ravaged, spirits burning, and fair Perushia enshrouded in Night Eternal.

For many minutes did I watch the breath of the graven image giving life to these visions of evil, all the time held in a state of great fear and intrigue. In time the visions within the smoke-like substance faded and the black cloud began swirling about dangerously, like a multitude of venomous black serpents dancing to the threnody of an unheard piper. These smoke phantoms stretched out to loom in menacing unison over the audience of tormented Undead, and then I beheld such a sight of intense cruelty, that I knew its origin could only lie within the malign mind of the *actual* Evil One! Every Undead corpse struggled violently against their restraints but none could escape the falling cloud of darkness as it entered their cold bodies. Then I could only be thankful of the ice wall separating me from the awful interior, for such was the expression of pain upon those faces of Undead flesh, that I knew the quality of their screams would have been horrendous but for the cold barrier's muffling.

As I walked away from that place of cruel suffering I again experienced many of those terrible visions I had just beheld, and I knew that dreadful place was the Volkh-Shar, The Pavilion of Nightmares Past.

Chapter XV
The Tower of the Torturer

Above the snow and ice its summit stands,
Brooding alone within the Frozen Lands.
Smooth as the polish of the mirror rise
Its slippery sides, and shoot into the skies.

It thrusts its spire into the ebon night
A shining shard of frozen, frosty white.
Crowned by a many-windowed cupola:
The tower of the Evil Akomar

Shalad Kazur, the Prophet of Kiran

AFTER SOME TIME of walking, my eyes beheld the sight of a slender white tower rising from the fields of ice and snow. Fashioned from the very frost, it rose into the dark skies of the Night Eternal and was featureless save at its top was a cupola fretted with many windows that looked out in all directions across this blighted land. However as I grew steadily nearer, I noticed a gate of utter blackness that stood at its base, and with this my approach became more cautious for even now malign eyes could be scrutinising my approach. As I drew nearer the black gate I saw it to be unlocked and unguarded, and this only served to fuel my curiosity further and gave me good hope of some shelter, for now my weakness and hunger were greater than I had ever known.

So I placed my hands upon the frosted bars of the black gate, wrought and twisted by magic into naked demons and Jinn dancing within tongues of flame, and though freezing pain then seared me I contrived to push the gate open sufficiently to allow me entrance to the strange tower.

For some little distance I walked along in almost total darkness then very suddenly the floor beneath my feet became brightly lit by a white radiance, which passed upward through a surface of crystalline frost. Looking about, I found myself inside a passageway not unlike that encountered within The Sea of Sadness, but this one had an aspect far more macabre. For upon its walls were flat bone shelves of great width, and these supported solid blocks of ice, and each block contained the body of a Heartbeat.

The deathly chill of the air in this place seemed colder than even the Frozen Plain without, for areas of white frost hung in the air like veils of observant mist. I looked upon the sombre faces of those encased within the ice, and evidence of their cold sorrow showed in salted tears having flowed from dolorous eyes, by tiny areas where the ice had melted. I knew these to be Heartbeats who had resisted the rule of the Dark Way, so that I became troubled at my lack of sympathy and sorrow for them. For were these not my brothers and should I not at this very moment be searching for the means to set them free?

I had walked deeper within the tower and after some while I came to a place where black veils hung down to shroud my view. So, very carefully I pulled the curtains apart and stepped through them, to stand at the foot of a staircase of ice, which spiralled upwards into the gloom. I began to climb the stairs and, after circling the tower but once, passed through another set of black veils to enter a large, dimly lit chamber; the floor here being completely fashioned of gleaming ice. I remained still for some while observing all that stood about me. At first I thought the floor to be covered with rows of crystalline coffins, but upon greater observation, saw each oblong casket to be shaped from ice.

Now, the sight I looked upon was very grim, for each coffin I saw was devoid of its lid, and this made it possible to observe that all were occupied. I drew closer to the nearest corpse, gazing down in silent study. Then I looked upon something that appalled but also captivated me with intrigue, for the body appeared to have grown deformed in a most hideous manner. I saw that the limbs of the corpse had somehow grown into the body, for just small stumps remained as arms and legs, giving the illusion I looked upon a wan, emaciated, human-like slug. Protruding from the pale skin of its chest, just above the heart, I saw two translucent tubes of crystal that led up into darkness; one of these appeared to be slowly extracting blood, while the other one gradually replaced it with a vile green fluid.

I walked through the cold gloom of the icy chamber, swirls of frost hanging round each casket like ghoulish vampires in spirit form, all delightedly surveying the results of their undead revelling. As I gazed down at the deformed bodies, it seemed my presence was perchance detected by some, for there would, on occasion, be a flicker of pale eyelids which would open slowly to display vacant eyes of a shocking red. Upon one occasion, flaking lips moved in an effort to communicate with me, but all that came forth was a series of unintelligible murmurings.

Eventually I came towards the back of the room, where I ascended a further set of stairs to another loftier chamber. This room was afforded light by an array of black candles, though the strange shapes and erratic flickerings of the shadows they threw seemed somehow very sinister to me. Then I beheld a sight which was uncanny and most unsettling, for in the centre of the circular chamber I saw a large crystal tank of emerald green fluid, and just visible within its jade depths, a collection of human heads. Into the top of each cranium was attached a small crystal tube which seemed to be steadily filtering a black fluid outwards; this I followed with my eyes and saw it led to a darkened area wherein stood another tank, smaller and not so easily perceivable. So I drew nearer to this dim-lit area, and was soon able to see that every tube slowly emptied the black fluid into this second container. This fluid, it seemed, appeared to struggle for release from its crystal prison, bubbling and splashing onto the sides as though terrified.

I looked back towards the heads in the larger tank, noting the expression of ultimate horror upon each countenance, and I entertained the bizarre notion that Fear itself had somehow been created and drawn from their minds. My curiosity at this idea became great, for such is the malign spell of this realm that it excites and nurtures the dark evil which exists within *every* man's heart, and I was but a victim of its strange intoxication and influence.

I noticed further shelves of bone; these were smaller and contained rows of sealed crystal jars, each holding varying quantities of struggling black fluid. For some time I paused and watched its frenzied efforts of escape, feeling strangely repelled but also excited. Then I left this chamber and continued ascending the stairway until the darkness became lit by the green glow of an archway.

Passing through this, I entered an area where white radiance rose from the walls and floor of ice to afford illumination, and the sight this presented caused me to gasp with utter shock and disbelief, for many deformed creatures now pushed themselves horizontally across the smooth surface of the floor, arms and legs no more than stumps which worked in unison to give a limited mobility. In certain areas I saw tomb-shaped holes had been gouged out of the ice, and these were full of plump Jazur Berries and culled corpse-meat, all savagely being devoured. Instantly I felt ravenous, so that all the shame and awareness of evil in my mind became temporarily brushed aside. After all, had I not eaten of such fare with the Mansion of Jeh? Truly it was so, and no harm had ensued.

I then walked across the ice in order to join with the other feasting creatures. Many snarled viciously, attacking me in the manner of jackals, and these I kicked at in wild anger until they came to a grudging acceptance of my presence. Then side-by-side we lowered our bodies to the icy trough and ate hungrily of the provender we found before us. But this time I offered *no* blessing to Zallah for those who had suffered that I might enjoy this repast, for hunger is no sin, and surely my quest was the will of Zallah?

* * *

It was as I was feasting from the trough, rotting flesh and clotted blood staining my lips, that I suddenly felt the touch of a cold bone hand grasp my hair and pull me to my feet. Then the cruel grip was relaxed and I was able to turn my head to see what new danger threatened. I beheld the sight of two black-shrouded Dead Ones. Without a whisper of sound they began to escort me forcibly over the ice, up yet another winding staircase and into an area shrouded in deepest darkness.

I know not how long I was marched through the pitch-blackness, circumnavigating the inside circumference of the tower, until eventually I came to approach a small area lit by the pale glow of a burning oil lamp. As I was led into this chamber I saw that I found myself within the interior of the cupola, for about the walls were myriad windows looking out into the ebon night. In this lofty room I saw a chair of twisted bone had been placed upon the ice, while before it, upon a small table, stood a crystalline goblet of blood, also of gleaming white bone. Very suddenly the Dead Ones released their grip upon me, and though I looked instantly to either side and down the staircase I had just ascended, I saw no sign of their retreating forms anywhere. It seemed they had vanished completely.

As I was now alone within the chamber I reasoned there was little danger if I were to sit down and rest for some while in the chair, for obviously I had been brought here for some purpose, and by now I had realised it was futile to resist the will of the Dead Ones. My heart felt empty for I now knew my very spirit and soul had been tainted beyond redemption, for I craved the crimson fluid set before me with every fibre of my being. Therefore, I leant forward and took the goblet of blood from the table, but as the very first drops of crimson passed my lips, there was the sudden flare of another lamp. And there, only yards before me sat the dreadful image of Akomar upon a chair, also of bone, an identical goblet of blood held in his own skeletal hand. I saw his pale lips, already stained with the red liquid, part slightly as he spoke.

"Welcome to my home Khalik. The Dark Way has claimed you body and soul. "

I knew I should have felt anger at these words, but instead I sipped again at the contents of the goblet.

"Now all that remains is the departure of your spirit, for the Sleeper in the Pavilion of Mystical Fire has great need of it. Admirably... your spirit has been shaped admirably. The Dark Way will know a final moulding and unification before the Healing takes place; you will cast off your body of death and let your spirit fly, for know you that your heart ceased to beat within the Frozen Plain! Now you shall know rebirth."

Before I could digest the import of his words Akomar stood up from his chair and walked towards me. One pale hand he placed over my face and the other grasped at the rear of my head; I felt the black talons of his fingers lacerate my skin as he began to apply pressure. Then I grew faint as he increased the pressure, his arms trembling such was the exertion.

Darkness came to me in an instant.

* * *

When vision returned, I found myself looking down upon my own discarded shell still seated upon the charnel throne. A cruel smile twisted the bloody mouth of Akomar, as he gazed upwards at my rising spirit and laughed a wicked laugh. I ascended still further, passing through ice and the vaulted ceiling of the cupola, then upward and away from the tower of Akomar into the glorious blackness of the Night Eternal!

Through dark skies I travelled, the moon's beams spilling over the landscape below me like silver rain and far below I beheld the Pavilion of Nightmares Past, so that I wondered if the blackened image of Zhariman was, even then, performing its macabre show. Onwards I travelled, to Ahlamdul, The Pyramid of Vile Intelligence; somehow it became aware of my passing, for briefly I heard the distant sound of its wailing siren and saw the eyes of each giant skull glow a deep red.

Soon I saw the ice giving way to the blackened earth and I knew that the ground concealed Pharezeum and Zirik Mobol, then I thought of the Faces of Torture that were forced to do the bidding of the Dark Way and I smiled. After a while, I saw the moon's beams pick out their sinister images in the darkness. Once more I travelled above the blackened earth, and I saw the presence of fire columns, glowing carriages of bone, sinister cathedrals, and I heard the baying of the Jat-Su.

There came to my ears one last dreadful howl as though a million dead screamed simultaneously, then everything was as silent as the spaces between the stars. I knew then that I approached The Valley of Mazrur. The eyes of The Watcher of The Valley opened, so that I could have sworn those green orbs of fire gazed angrily skywards, annoyed at the presence of one who had once traversed its forbidden vale. Then I saw the Perfumed Gardens of Death, with the moon's rays briefly highlighting that awful figure stood upon the Balcony of Night.

Then I beheld the tomb-shaped houses in Jilyah, and even as I passed I witnessed some poor wretch being dragged through the streets by the Dead Ones. Yet still I soared onwards, and very suddenly my ears were filled with dreadful screams while the landscape below glowed with searing flame and I knew I passed over the horrendous Fields of Atesh Ghah.

And soon I saw Vouruskasha, The Sea of Sadness, with countless mist-wreathed spirits of the dead dancing upon its roiling surface, all to unheard threnodies of evil. Then I saw the moon's beams highlight the dome of the Pavilion of Sunrise, and I saw its walls were still devoid of colour, so that I thought sorrowfully of Changra Bel and his childish shadows. After a time I passed above the chasm of Sindroo, where Yindra sat concealed beneath the bridge of Zinvat, and it seemed he raised his eyes towards me and smiled in wicked satisfaction. But I passed him by and soon I found myself above The Valley of The Shadows, and it was here that I began a slow descent.

Upon the ridge at the far end of the valley stood Atesh Yarnath, The Pavilion of Mystical Fire, yet I realised that something was now very wrong, for this pavilion which had burned through all the dark of eternity was dying. But still I found myself descending from the black sky, down, down, through the very roof of the building, my spirit entering the damaged mind of

the Sleeper within, becoming one with it and displacing its own fragile spirit.
   Then I slept.

Chapter XVI
Ereshkiga: Shadowqueen

When darkness falls and creatures call from under crimson skies,
Upon the ravaged breeze the savage demons ride.
And I will sink into the darkness of your eyes.

When you awaken you will think it just a dream,
But your soul has been taken by, the Shadowqueen.

The Songs of Jhal, Volume XIX

I KNEW SOMETHING OR someone had entered the chamber and awakened me. Darkness hung all about me, there was just a faint radiance from the floor to bring a shred of comfort to my bemused mind, and from beside the carpets of my bed the slightest glow from the strangest, wilting, flower. Confusion filled me, I searched my tattered mind for a shred of returning memory -- but found little. My very identity seemed to have been lost to the black skies I had passed through, and now my stolen spirit felt as if it had been *moulded* to another's, though still in a state of extreme weakness.

All I knew was that a silent but undeniable presence of evil had awakened me from my slumber and now, blurry eyed, I searched the deepest shadows of the chamber with an infinite dread of what I may find. And fearfully I gasped, for my eyes came to focus on the outline of some sinister figure, standing merged with the darkness of a deeply shadowed corner.

Seconds passed in unearthly silence, my eyes slowly making out the shrouded figure, while the merest suggestion of yellowed bone began to displace the haunting blackness of a cowl. Suddenly, in the threatening silence of the chamber, a voice spoke out. It was a voice of a dry, unused quality; like a voice from beyond the tomb.

"Your presence is demanded; the Healer has summoned you! "

Slowly the malign figure began to move, and as it drew closer to me, I knew the charnel stench of its putrid, rotting flesh and in my mind I heard a thousand dark sighs from the long-buried dead, and the undying screams of souls sentenced to an everlasting damnation. Cold arms reached out to clasp my body in a macabre embrace, and I was lifted from my carpets with unnatural ease. Still within the arms of that evil visitant, I was moved towards and *through* the walls of the pavilion, for barriers hold no substance for the will of the dead.

Amidst the perpetual dark, I was taken to the outer night; suspended in the air like the helpless prey of some black, demonic bat-winged Jinni. But as I was moved in the direction of some fearful, unknown destination, a vague remembrance came to me. And with this came the thought: Who are *you* to take liberties with one such as I?

With a movement more of instinct than thought, I moved my hands swiftly upwards and onto that grim face of bone. At once the silence of the night shattered with a scream like that of a tortured Utukku, and at my touch, the semblance of long-dead bone before me crumbled to dust.

* * *

Through the night I fell, though slowly as in a dream, and in time landed upon a dismal, black-sanded landscape. About me grew sporadic groupings of small, stunted trees and bushes, and above, in the black void of mystery, there hung the palest of moons gazing down upon my sorrowful plight with a wan face of pity. Then, as I gazed upwards, the whitened surface shimmered, and it seemed, that a hollow-eyed visage stared back from that blanched orb, and from the empty sockets trickled tears of blood...

Beneath me, a darkened valley was home to a thousand shadows, though it came as a mystery to me which objects threw these shadows, unless perchance it was the moon's glow upon the occasional trees -- but this I thought unlikely. And from this place came a sense of ill will that rose upwards, pervading my soul, while my spirit became infected by the awesome isolation. And so, I then began to retrace my path, for though I disremembered much, surely the house I'd slept in had been my home. So onwards I walked through that dark, desolate place, until my eyes came to look upon the pavilion of my memory's origin. But with this sight I plunged into a dark abyss of despair, for the lower half of the building was entirely aflame.

So with haste I ran towards that object of all my hopes, and as I drew closer, I saw that even the upper stonework was black and charred; as though fire had once engulfed the entire house, burning with a much greater fury than it did at present. And this enigma I could not fathom. Then, as I approached the outer walls, I noticed a small window that remained oddly intact despite the intense heat. Peering inside I beheld a black-cloaked figure walking slowly through the inner flames. Through his magical powers, the figure suddenly became aware of my prying eyes, and turning quickly, came to face in my direction. Immediately, I drew back from the window, afraid of that strange occupant defying the fires of a certain death. But still my eyes saw within, and though the swirling smoke disguised the face of the occupant, still I saw the arm rise towards me -- with the motion of beckoning.

And what choice did I have but to obey that terrifying summons, for the only knowledge I held, was knowing this bizarre pavilion to be in some way linked to myself. Walking to the front of the building, I found a strange door which seemed in a state of perpetual burning; but now the *inner* fires of my bewildered mind burnt with a curiosity transcending all barriers: I was now prepared to exchange my existence for the revelation of my own identity.

The door opened at a push, and so I entered the eternal flames of the pavilion. But as I stood amid that broiling furnace, the pain and suffering I had been prepared for did not come. Instead, those savage flames licked about me like elemental pets, creating endearing displays of affection for their master.

And still my flesh did not burn!

Through the flames, I saw the black-cloaked figure moving towards me; with its slow advance came a steady dispersion of smoke about the face. But with the revelation of the countenance came a riot of churning emotion in me. For though the smile was of sweet feminine welcome, the black and charred remnants of the face were repulsive beyond imagining. Her cracked lips moved and she spoke:

"I am Ereshkiga, the Shadowqueen."

Then she moved towards me with arms outstretched, and I could not turn away, for I knew there to be a genuine love in her dark embrace. And as those black charred lips pressed softly against my own, my mouth opened in eagerness for her burning breath to enter.

I stared deep into her ruined face, searching for the answers to a million questions.

"Who am I? " I asked.

"I cannot tell you," she replied, "for He has summoned you, and I cannot intervene. "

I felt an immense fatigue wash over me.

"I am too tired to leave this place. I wish only to sleep; to sleep in this pavilion. "

She walked through the flames to stand before a burning shelf of crystal jars. Inside each, a black substance seemed to struggle for release. I watched as she selected one of the largest, returning to me with it.

"What is it? " I asked.

"It is the Wine of the Shadows of Night, " she replied.

"And the others?"

"They are all the results of your great work, my love.""

She uncorked the jar and held it out to me.

"Drink the Wine of the Shadows of Night and you will feed on their terror! "

I lifted the jar to my lips, pouring the foul-smelling contents inside my mouth. And as the cold substance slid down my throat, it seemed a thousand screams of torment filled my mind, and with this I grew strong and derived much pleasure from the multitude of panicked voices. For I knew that *I* was the cause of all their dread.

Once more that blackened face looked upon my own. Then as I gazed back the scorched flesh began to writhe and twist as muscle and skin reformed. Within moments the visage of Ereshkiga was disclosed. Truly this revelation was the most staggering sight I had yet beheld and my mind reeled in profound shock, for I looked upon the face of a woman of wondrous beauty. And, though it meant nothing to me, my mind echoed with the name Zareena... Zareena... Zareena.

Smiling, she revealed sharp, pointed teeth and slowly stretched out her hands, softly cupping my face between them. Her newly formed, soft red lips planted a kiss upon my own.

"So, Khalik my love, we are united at last! Shaizan awaits you."

Her words puzzled me.

"I will go to him." I replied.

* * *

Leaving the flaming pavilion I walked downwards, for Ereshkiga had told me I must cross the Valley of the Shadows and go onwards to The Cave from Where the Dead Ones Walk. And over the entire valley hung a deathly spell of silence, only broken at times by the eerie sighs of the wind. Then, when I came to the bottom of the valley, that sense of ill will again pervaded me; it felt as though some unseen intelligence tried to possess my mind. A multitude of grotesque, black shadows populated the entire floor of the valley, and as I walked, certain ones appeared to be matching my steady progress with their own stealthy movement.

Suddenly I heard sounds, as of whispering voices in the night.

"He has forgotten!" said one voice.

"No, it cannot be, it is merely a trick. He wishes to steal our---"

"Hush!" came another voice, "If he has forgotten, then I will..." But the rest of the words I could not hear.

As I continued onwards, a coldness and sense of fatigue began to creep over me. Suddenly I found it hard to draw breath; a choking sensation filled my throat. Turning round quickly, I found a shadow following close behind; somehow its hands had clasped themselves about my neck. At once I struck out in defence, but the dark form I struggled with held no substance. Like a vision from my past came a remembrance from the very last dregs of memory, it was the voice of my forgotten existence: "Protect yourself, you *know* how!"

Instinctively I opened my mouth and a sound issued forth into the darkness. It was the voice of the darkest of nights; of a wild ghul howling; of the last pleading thoughts of all frightened, dying men and women. And as though trapped by a force of evil, the shadow who had tried to do me harm was drawn by the source of the dark sound; imprisoned by the scream, and sucked deep into my lungs, replenishing my soul.

I closed my mouth and the sound ceased abruptly.

"It was as I said -- a trick," said a voice.

I will have you all!" I bellowed. And with this came further murmurs of fear, as throughout the valley opened a pathway free of shadow.

* * *

Reaching the termination of the valley, I began to climb upwards over the hard gritstone rock towards The Cave From Where The Dead Ones Walk. I saw their black-shrouded forms about the mouth of the cavern, and vaguely wondered what work of evil the hands of the dead did perform. As I neared the cave, I saw their heads turn slowly in my direction, and with this came a realisation that they awaited me. Soon those hooded figures approached me, three standing each side, so that I was given no recourse but to be accompanied into the darkness of the cave by this macabre escort. I walked onwards through the pitch-blackness, the stench and coldness from their rotting bodies coming as a reminder of their nearness. But soon I detected a glimmer of light. And with time there grew upon my sight the vision of a large underground amphitheatre.

I stepped out from the darkness and into the glare of fire-torches, but the sight they afforded made me freeze in a stance of total fear. All around the theatre stood tiers of stone slabs and shattered mortuary blocks, which led up into an eventual darkness. Occasional black-shrouded figures could be seen, laid in unnatural stillness like sleeping scorpions. But in the centre of the amphitheatre was an image of such dark extravagance as would stun the very soul. For in full illumination of the fire-torches stood a macabre lake of blood, and knelt at the edge was a sickening figure, black and horned, whose tongue lapped thirstily at the redness. But now my observations ceased abruptly as my insistent escorts moved me onwards towards the stone slabs.

And there I was left alone, seated on the frontal tier of those slabs, again having the vision of the crimson lake before my eyes. After a while, my departed memory began to stir, and it came to me that my eyes now looked upon Ibliz, the Lake of Shaizan -- so that I shuddered with the knowledge. Suddenly I noticed a disturbance at the far edge of the lake, a bubbling and splashing of blood in frantic fashion, as though something fought in a desperate attempt *not* to surface.

And with a speed far beyond thought, I saw two of the black-shrouded dead pluck some smooth, white, struggling *Thing* from that bloodied lake of evil. Then a scream filled the air; a scream of unparalleled fear and dread, which reclaimed more of my tattered memory, for somehow I knew the white visage I looked upon, was that of a human soul! With this, I almost grew ashamed, for I *laughed*; I laughed and felt good about the suffering I saw. Still within the grasp of the dead, that tortured soul was taken to a shadowed area where darkened steps led downwards and I saw it no more.

The sinister figure beside the lake had ceased drinking, and now gazed upon me in dark scrutiny. The vile creature was twice the height of a man and as it stood and walked over to me, I noticed for the first time that it was cloven hoofed, and my terror was deep and sublime. Coming to a halt just before me, its dark eyes seemed to penetrate my soul.

"Who are you?" I asked.

A stained red tongue flicked over bloodied lips.

"You know me. I am Shaizan, Lord of Darkness."

"What do you want with me?"

"It is time for your awakening, the Night Eternal has moulded your soul; you are prepared."

At this, huge black-taloned hands manoeuvred me; laying me out upon the stone slab. The ebon leather-like skin creased as He knelt over me, His worm-like questing tongue travelling over my face to lick my eyes. Then His mouth touched my own and opened for a torrent of warm revitalising blood to transfer between us. I drank thirstily: deeply. Tearing carefully at his own body, His talons tore strips of raw flesh from His vast chest. These he then placed over my face and with deft movements moulded His flesh with mine. Then he spoke:

"Flesh of my flesh I give to you."

Then his scimitar-like talons sliced into my very skull, but of pain I felt none. A warm sensation flooded my being: sensuous and comforting. I knew that the facile hands of Shaizan were deftly moulding my thoughts for I was now a creature of the Night Eternal. I rejoiced in the loving caress of Shaizan and when all was done, evil pulsed through me once more -- and I *knew* who I was!

Chapter XVII
Zhariman, the Demon Lord

"'t'is said the soul of mortal man recoiled
To view Black Shaizan's eye, so fierce and wild.
Vast talons, foul with human flesh, there grew
    In place of hands, and features of an ebon hue
Glar'd in His visage, whilst the obscene waist
    Warm skins of human victims close embraced.

The Shah Nurmal, Book X

I ROSE UP FROM the slab and gazed upon my Lord and Creator. I bowed to Him and kissed the ground between my hands. Then, summoning the Dead Ones with a gesture I left the cavern and walked down into The Valley of Shadows. I glanced up at the sickly moon and it almost seemed; yes it seemed that the pale white orb held a countenance of grim satisfaction.

In time I arrived at The Pavilion of Nightmares, which I knew to be my home and, dismissing the Dead Ones entered the dwelling. Flames licked and caressed me as I walked for their Master had returned. Then, from an adjoining chamber a figure emerged, the enveloping flames parting like silk veils to reveal the form of a female.

"Zareena?" The name came unbidden to my lips, though I knew of none by that name, for I retained no memory of my dead love.

"No! Not Zareena! That mortal fool exists no longer. I am Ereshkiga, the Shadowqueen, and you my love..."

"I," I interrupted, "I am Zhariman, the Demon, Lord of the Night Eternal!"

Smiling a smile of pure evil Ereshkiga moved towards me and clasped me within her alabaster arms.

"We are together at last my Lord. You have realised your destiny and embraced the Dark Way. Now we shall rule the everlasting Night Eternal from our thrones of blackened bone and the screams of the tormented shall be as heady wine and intoxicate our senses."

I embraced my Queen of Shadows, and kissed her poisoned lips. Then I raised my fist to the black, funeral vault of the cryptic heavens and shouted:

"These are the days of Falling Night when Shaizan, The Evil One, our Lord and Father shall harvest the souls of all mankind. The demon hordes shall awaken and their howling shall rise to the very Heavens. The air shall darken and the Earth shall grow black and men's eyes will be enveloped in shadows. Monsters, demons and Jinn shall flow from the darkness, attracted by the stench of humanity, to frolic and feed in the death lands of perpetual night."

And at my command the Shadow Creatures of delirious nightmare began to rise from up their lairs and darkness dripped from the skies . . .

APPENDIX I
A GLOSSARY OF PERUSHIA

Ahlamdul: The Pyramid of Vile Intelligence that stands deep within the Frozen Plain.
Akomar the Torturer: Creator of the various methods of vile torture and torment within The Night Eternal. Also known as Alazaar the Showman.
Alazaar The Showman: He provides the entertainment inside the Pavilion of Pleasure and Pain in the village of Jilyah. He is also known as Akomar, The Torturer.
Al Ishakar: Father of the Caliph Al-Kalooor, he was the fifth Caliph of Sharador.
Al-Kaloor: Father of the Caliph Al-Pharazeme, he was the sixth Caliph of Sharador.
Al Pharazeme: The seventh Caliph of Sharador. The evil Caliph was once a fair and just ruler and the land of Perushia prospered under his reign. But he was corrupted by the guile of the Evil One and, in the Days of Falling Darkness, became a cruel and wicked demon.

Arallu: Evil genii that issue from the Night Eternal. They heed neither prayer nor supplication

Atesh Ghah, The Fields of: An area of charred earth and great erupting fissures of flame. In this land of fire and destruction there are countless stakes upon which hang the tormented bodies of the burning undead.

Atesh Yarnath: The Pavilion of Mystical Fire that stands upon an outcropping of rock in the Shadow Mountains and looks out over Yarna, the Valley of Shadows.

Ayohsust: In Perushian mythology a river of fire. Azi Dahka the Storm God was consumed in its flames.

Azi Dahka: In Perushian mythology a storm god. He was consumed in the flames of Ayohsust, the River of Fire.

Azmaraz: In Perushian mythology the Angel of Silence.

Baul: Perushian god of the moon; also a name for the moon itself.

Balcony of Night: Located in the Perfumed Gardens of Death. Mashyane, the Dark-Minded Mother of Death stands here and gazes out over the nightmares of men.

Berries of Death: See *Jazur Berries*.

Book of Shamash, The: A Perushian book of mythology written by the legendary poet Shamash.

Caliph: the office, rank, government or empire of a caliph

Cave From Where The Dead Ones Walk, The: See *Uruk-atil*.

Chamberlain: An officer appointed by a king or nobleman.

Changra Bel: The Man of Visions. He dwells within Shamash, the Pavilion of Sunrise.

Concubine: An unmarried woman living with a man.

Courtesan: A court mistress; a whore; a woman of the court.
Crimson Breath: The *Vapours of Purification* which ever pour from the *Pool of Purification*.
Crimson River of Death: See *Zirik Mobol*.
Daevas - In Perushian mythology they are demons who cause plagues and diseases and who fight every form of religion. They are devoted to trickery and falsehood. Their vocation is to thwart all efforts to achieve good. They are the male servants of Zhariman. The female servants are called the Drujs.
Dark Minded Mother of Death, The: See *Mashyane*.
Dead Ones, The: Dark, shrouded figures of death, they are the servitors of The Demon Lord.
Dervish: a poor man
Desert of Desolation, The: See *Shendi*.
Dirzeem: a weight or silver coin
Drujs: Female demons: creatures of deceit and monstrous appearance. They are the female servants of Zhariman. The male servants are called the Daevas.
Dungeons of Al Pharazeme: Extensive dungeons below the palace of Al Pharazeme. Within their borders lies an entranceway to The Night Eternal.
Edimmu: the souls of the dead. They avenge themselves by tormenting the living.
Emir: An independent chieftain.
Ereshkiga: Princess of the Night Eternal and concubine to Zhariman. Together they do the bidding of their Lord Shaizan and rule The Night Eternal. She is also known as The Shadowqueen.
Fakir: a religious wonder worker
Fire Salamanders: Black lizards the size of dogs with red and yellow star markings along their backs. They live in

pools of fire and molten rock. Their skin secretes a toxin that burns and shrivels human skin on contact; the flesh withers instantly to the bone until only a blackened, shrunken corpse is left.

Frozen Plain, The: See *Kuruk Kulla*

Gandarewa: A water demon that lives in a coral palace beneath the Sea of Sadness.

Genii: See *Jinni*

Ghul: A ghoul; a carrion creature that resembles a hybrid of man and jackal and feasts upon the rotting flesh of corpses. They are often to be found haunting the cemeteries and tombs of the dead. They possess a cunning intelligence and are formidable adversaries if cornered.

Ghulh: A female Ghul; they are most difficult to tell apart from their male counterparts as they share the same appearance and habits.

Ghost of Sorrows, The: See *Rahyani*.

Giaour: Infidel

Grand Vizir: Prime Minister and commander of the army.

Grandee: A man of high rank; a noble.

Gorannon: The Skull-Lit Bridge Of Evil. A bridge of whitened bone that spans Zirik Mobol; it stands deep within the dungeons of Al Pharazeme.

Harakash: A land of Perushia

Healing of Al Pharazeme, The: It was said that the Evil One granted Al Pharazeme the boon of eternal life, though some says it was more like an eternal death.

Houris: The Virgins of Paradise.

Ibliz: The lake of Shaitan, the Evil One. It consists entirely of blood.

Illonia: A land of Perushia.

Inner Orb: A mystical orb by which means it is possible to traverse both space and time within the realm of The Night Eternal. It is in the possession of Changra Bel in Shamash, the Pavilion of Sunrise.

Ishakkar: A Perushian city

Jaristan: A land visited by Khalik the sailor on his ninth voyage it lies far to the east of Perushia in the Zinnamon Sea.

Jat-Su: The black Night Hounds that roam the dark wastelands on The Night Eternal, their snouts a quiver for the scent of untainted souls.

Jalur the Demon: Slave and assistant to Alazaar the showman.

Jazur Berries: The Berries of Death. They grow in the land of the Night Eternal and are berries about the size of a pomegranate. Their skin is rotting human flesh and their pulp is congealed blood.

Jeh: The whore. In Perusian mythology, she is responsible for the death of the first man Rhazor, because she poisoned him at the instigation of Zhariman. She dwells within the Mansion of Evil

Jilyah: The village of the Heartbeats.

Jinn/Jinni: Spirits formed of fire living chiefly in the mountains of Kaffor, which circle the world. They assume various shapes, sometimes men of enormous size.

Jinniyah: A Female Jinn

Keseva: The *Pool of Purification,* which separates body and soul. It sands within the Tombs of Torture beneath the palace city of Sharador.

Khalik: A sailor and adventurer and the hero of many tales. He entered The Night Eternal to rescue Zareena, the daughter of the Caliph Al Pharazeme.

Khostrau: Magician and conjurer to the court of Al Pharazeme.
Kiran: A small island off the western coast of Perushia. Home of the ancient prophet Shalad Kazur.
Kuruk Kulla: the Frozen Plain. A vast expanse of ice and snow to the north of Pharezeum.
Man Of Visions: See Changra Bel.
Mansion of Evil: Dwelling place of Jeh the Whore.
Maruk-Lith: the Watcher of the Valley. His unsleeping gaze forever sweeps the darkness of the Vale of Mazrur.
Mashyane: The Dark Minded Mother of Death. She perceives all from her Balcony of Night and stalks the dreams of men with nightmares at her heels.
Maymunah: Daughter of the King of the Jinn
Vale of Mazrur, The: The Dread Valley of Silence, watched over by Maruk Lith, the Watcher of the Valley.
Mazura Aharza - In Perusian belief, Mazura Aharza ("Lord Wisdom") was the supreme god, he who created the heavens and the Earth. It is said he wrote the *Shah Nurmal – The Book of Demons.*
Mullah: A teacher.
Parasang: Between 3 and 4 miles.
Pavilion of Mystical Flame: See *Atesh Yarnath*.
Pavilion of Nightmares Past: See *Volkh-Shar*.
Pavilion of Pleasure and Pain: A place of entertainment for the Heartbeats dwelling within the village of Jilyah.
Pavilion of Sunrise: See *Shamash*.
Perfumed Gardens of Pleasure, The: The lush, exotic gardens of the Caliph Al Pharazeme, filled with rare plants, shrubs and trees collected by his sorcerers from all corners of Perushia. It was the favourite trysting place for Khalik and Zareena.
The Perfumed Gardens of Death: See *Rahyani*

Peris: Perusian spirits of great beauty who guide mortals on their way to the Land of the Blessed. They also battle the Daevas.

Plains of Rudah: A plain of perpetual mist and silence. It stands on the northern side of the chasm of Sindroo.

Pool of Purification, The: See *Keseva*.

Pharezeum: - the Port of Death, it lies upon the Crimson River of Death.

Pyramid of Vile Intelligence, The: See *Ahlamdul*.

Rahyani: The Ghost of Sorrows. She weeps eternally within the Perfumed Gardens of Death.

Raja - A prince or king.

Ranu: God of the sky. He reigned over the heavens. He was the supreme god and never left the heavenly region.

Rea: God of the water.

Ruz Shamral: They have the appearance of orange orbs of flame, but are the charred skulls of humans constantly burning. They have the gift of flight and within The Night Eternal they herd the undead, at the bidding of the vile intelligence within the pyramid Alhamdul.

Saal: A hero of the ancient Perushian epics.

Samarzul - A land bordering Perushia to the north.

Seraglio: A harem, a collection of wives

Shadowqueen: See *Ereshkiga*

Shah-Nurmal: The Book of Demons. It contains stories and poems concerning the heroes of Perushian mythology including much on The Night Eternal. It also includes the legends of Zal in the Land of Demons.

Shamash: The Pavilion of Sunrise. It stands upon a headland that juts out into Vouruskasha, The Sea of Sadness. It is the dwelling of Changra Bel.

Shaizan: The Lord of Darkness and creator of The Night Eternal. Zhariman is his creation also, brought into being to rule The Night Eternal and the denizens of darkness.

Shalad Kazur: The Prophet of Kiran. He wrote much in the Shah Nurmal concerning The Night Eternal

Sharador: Fabulous city of rare delights, Sharador is the capital city and crowning jewel of all of Perushia.

Shendi: The Desert of Desolation. A vast wasteland of empty night.

Shotu: The Tunnel of Darkness. Means by which the river Zirik Mobol flows from the realm of Perushia into The Night Eternal.

Sindroo: A bottomless chasm that divides The Night Eternal. It can only be crossed by means of the bridge Zinvat which is guarded by the demon Yindra.

Sister Midnight: A female vampire who haunts the village of Jilyah preying on its inhabitants.

Skull-lit Bridge of Evil: See *Gorannon*.

Songs of Jhal, The: Jhal was a poet and musician to the Caliph Shandral Khal, ruler of the ancient lost city of Iskanadul. His twenty-eight volumes of songs now repose in the Great Library of Perushia.

Sultan: A ruler.

Suzerain: A sovereign.

Sultana: a lady of a Sultan's harem; a king's mistress; a magnificent courtesan; a concubine.

Suloman: In Perushian mythology an ancient and wise ruler who sat upon a throne of beaten gold flanked by two panthers of ebony and jade.

Surya: In Perushian mythology the God of the Blazing Sun. He lives in the great Mountain of the East defended by the scorpion men and rides his chariot across the skies to the Mountain of the West

Thanarbul: A far land of steaming jungles whence came the snake-haired, scaled-skinned female dancers of Al Pharazeme's court.

Tombs of Torture: Vast dungeons beneath the Palace of Sharador, built, at the request of Al-Pharazeme, by demons and Jinn at the command of Zhariman. It is said they abut The Night Eternal itself.

Tunnel of Darkness, The: See *Shotu*.

Ulasto Vidath: The Corpse Keeper; the Harvester of Souls. The Perushian demon of death from which no human escapes. He Catches the souls of the dead and is ancient beyond remembering. He is lord of Rahyani: The Perfumed Gardens of Death.

Uruk-atil: A cave with a great mountain at the northern edge of the Valley of Shadows. Within lies the realm of the Dead Ones.

Valley of Shadows: See Yarna.

Vapours of Purification: Vapours that rise from Keseva the Pool of Purification.

Varuni: A concubine of the Caliph's seraglio. Her likeness was used by a Peri to trick Khalik into eating the provender of the Demon Lord.

Village of Heartbeats, The: See *Jilyah*.

Volkh-Shar: The Pavilion of Nightmares Past in which the undead are tormented by the evil visions of Shaizan.

Vouruskasha - The Sea of Sadness. A vast sea at the centre of The Night Eternal.

Wazir: A Vizier.

White Flower of Death, The: See *White Lotus of Decay*

White Lotus of Decay: A single white lotus that emanates a mystical radiance. Also known as The White Flower of Death.

Wine of the Shadows of Night: Also known as the Broth of Fear. It is the distillation of absolute fear into a black liquid.
Yarna: The Valley of Shadows. It lies within The Night Eternal.
Yindra: The Jinni which hides beneath the bridge of Zinvat in the chasm Sindroo. He stands thrice the height of a man and has skin of crimson hue, great black, bat-like wings, twisted horns, wicked fangs and evil amber eyes.
Zal In The Land of Demons: Epic saga concerning the heroic warrior Zal and his exploits in the Land of Demons.
Zallah: The God of the Perushian faith.
Zaraby: A land bordering Perushia to the east.
Zareena: The only daughter of the Evil Caliph, Al Pharazeme and beloved of Khalik the adventurer.
Zhariman: In Perusian religion Zhariman is the god of darkness, the eternal destroyer of good, personification and creator of evil, bringer of death and disease. His name means "fiendish spirit". He is the Demon Lord of the Night Eternal where he lives in perpetual darkness. To this place all those who do evil go to after their demise and suffer eternal suffering and damnation. His symbol is the snake. He is seen as the personification of evil, and will lead the dark forces against the hosts of mankind in the final days of Perushia. His Lord and Master is Shaizan.
Zinshaz: The disguise adopted by The Demon Lord, Zhariman to infiltrate the court of the Caliph Al Pharazeme and corrupt him with his guileful and wicked ways. He was granted the gift of becoming Grand Vizier after preparing a fine meal for the Caliph.

Zinvat: The bridge which spans the bottomless chasm of Sindroo. Any who would cross the bridge would be seized by the demon Yindra lying in wait beneath the bridge and cast into the gulf below.

Zirik Mobol - The Crimson River of Death that flows beneath the city of Sharador and into the realm of The Night Eternal. It is a river of blood.

Zohar: In Perushian mythology Zohar was a Caliph who was cursed by the Demon Lord and persuaded to kill his father. Every day serpents sprang from his shoulders, to be cut away and reappear the following day.

Appendix II
The Cartography of Perushia

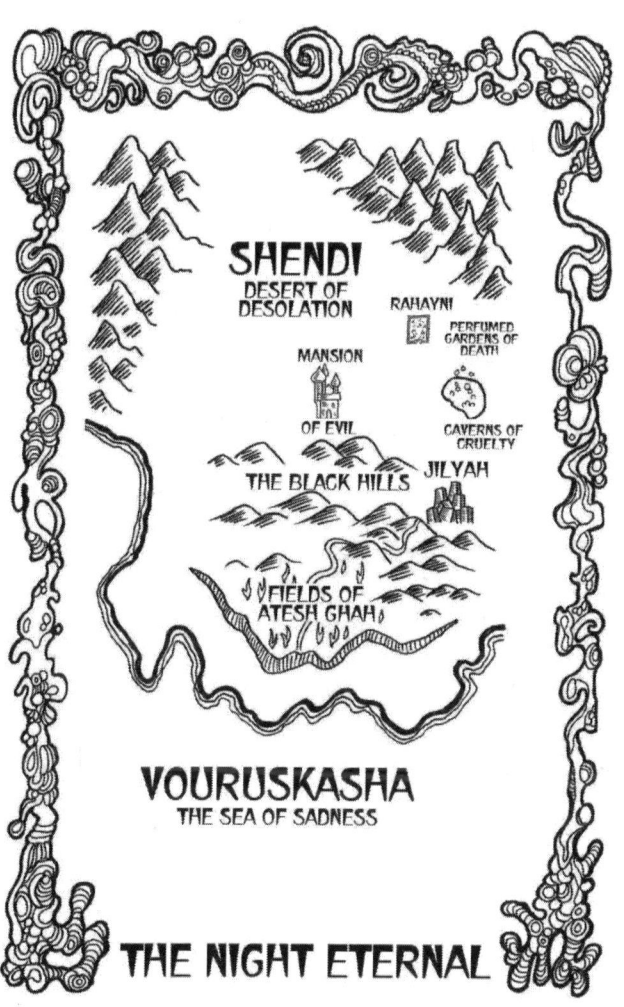

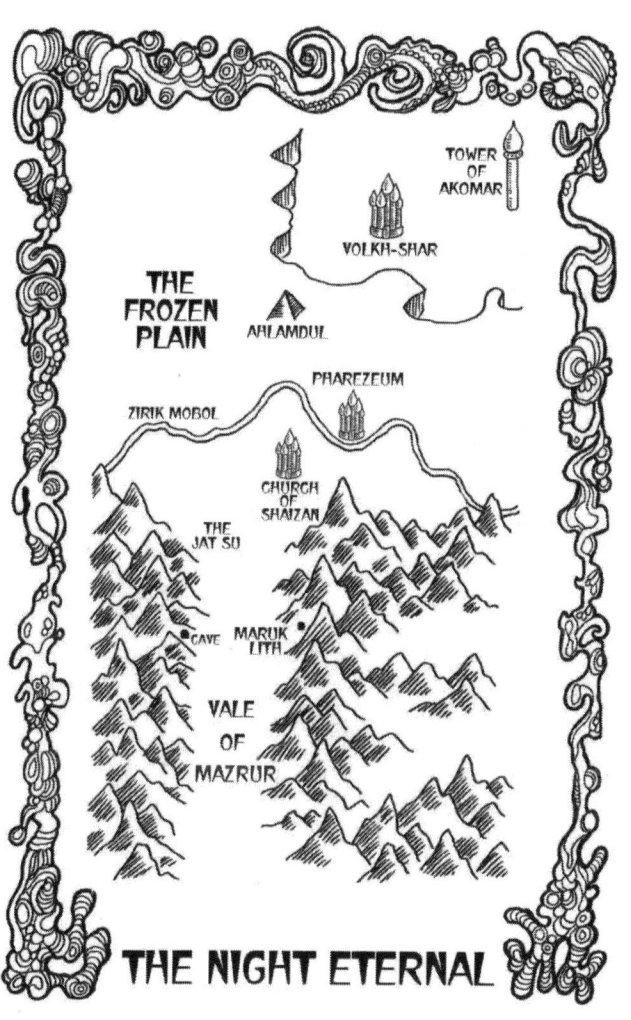

Acknowledgements: Our eternal thanks go to Bruce Pennington for allowing us to use his fantastic art for the cover, Clive Jones for the proofreading and Paul Edwards for his invaluable help in putting this book together.

Printed in Dunstable, United Kingdom